Cheaper by The Coven

Kitty Coven Book 3

Celeste Hall

Copyright © 2014 Celeste Hall

All rights reserved.

ISBN: 9798423654740

No part of this book may be reproduced, scanned, or distributed in any printed or electronic form without permission. Please do not participate in or encourage piracy of copyrighted materials in violation of the author's rights. Please purchase only authorized editions.

This book is a work of fiction. Names, characters, places, and incidents either are products of the author's imagination or are used fictitiously. Any resemblance to actual events or locales or persons, living or dead, is entirely coincidental.

DEDICATION

This series is dedicated to my amazing "Katie-Cat". Ever since she was a little girl, she was always bringing home stray felines. Despite being scratched, bitten, peed on, and a mild case of ringworm, she has never met a cat that she hasn't liked. If anyone deserves to find happily ever after in the arms of a handsome werecat, it's her!

CONTENTS

Chapter One   1

Chapter Two   16

Chapter Three   22

Chapter Four   33

Chapter Five   43

Chapter Six   53

Chapter Seven   58

Chapter Eight   66

Chapter Nine   73

Chapter Ten   81

🐈 CHAPTER ONE

Heidi woke up with a jolt, her naked body bathed in sweat, and her heart thundering wildly in her chest.

It took several long moments before she was able to calm down, even after she'd turned on the bedside lamp and was assured that she was safe and sound, and all alone in her comfortable king-sized bed.

"Crap," she growled softly. The nightmares were back, and they were worse than ever. Even after so many months of therapy, the memory of being held captive and beaten for over seventy-two hours still haunted her.

Maybe it because she was rapidly approaching the two-year anniversary of those horrific days.

Crawling out of bed, she padded across the floor of her open loft apartment and poured herself a glass of water from the pitcher in the fridge.

From where she now stood, she could see every corner of the spacious floorplan, including the area designated for the bathroom, with its heavy claw-foot tub. She could soak in that tub for hours and never worry about someone sneaking up on her from another room.

There was a small, closeted area for the toilet, but otherwise, the closest thing to a visual barrier was the old-fashioned folding dressing screen, which could be used if she had guests over.

However, the only guests she ever really allowed here were her two best friends, Rachel and Morgan. Occasionally, one of their boyfriends tried to join the girls. But when that happened, Heidi usually found an excuse to move the group to a more neutral territory, like her favorite bar.

This apartment was Heidi's sanctuary, a place for her to retreat from the world and feel safe. A mandatory expense after Morgan's ex-boyfriend, Craig, had experienced a drug-induced psychotic break and took both Morgan and Heidi hostage.

Morgan had frozen in fear and pain, curling into a silently sobbing ball to avoid his wrath. But Heidi had panicked and fought back. A mistake which had earned her a cracked rib, three broken fingers, two black eyes, a concussion, and a whole lot of scrapes and bruises.

It had taken months for her to heal physically, but the emotional and psychological wounds were still raw.

For a while she'd relied upon her friends to help her through the bad days. But they both had steady men in their lives now, and neither of them really understood how deeply the event had scarred her, or how those scars still affected her daily life.

Part of that was probably Heidi's fault. She didn't like showing weakness, so she'd put on a brave face and made jokes to distract her friends from the truth. She knew that if she called them, they'd have dropped everything and come to offer their support, but she didn't want to disrupt their happiness.

Stalking back over to the bed, she let herself fall into the rumpled sheets and mattress with a heavy sigh. It was wasted effort. A glance at the little clock on her bedside table, warned that she had less than an hour before she needed to get up and get ready for work.

It would be useless trying to go back to sleep now. By

the time her nerves were settled enough for her to drift off, the alarm would wake her up again.

With a sigh, she crawled out of the bed and tugged open one of the two large, freestanding wardrobes, which served as the support beams for a long, double rack of dresses and blouses.

The wardrobes contained the items she didn't want left on display, like intimate apparel, t-shirts and sweats. She pulled on a set of the last two now and tugged a baseball cap down over a messy ponytail.

A quick check in the full-length mirror assured that the outfit wasn't going to win her any fashion awards, but she could still pull off that sexy Jock look, which had made her such a popular cheerleader back during high school.

Ages ago.

Whatever happened to that spunky, fearless girl?

"She grew up and realized that life could be a real bitch," she answered herself.

Shoving her feet into a pair of sneakers, she left the apartment and jogged down thirteen flights of stairs to the underground parking level. The community gym was squirreled away in one corner here and was rarely used at this early hour.

Whenever she found it difficult to be alone with her thoughts, it helped to come down and give herself something else to think about. There was nothing like the burn from a hard workout to rid her of any unwanted stress or fear. As well as any extra weight she might have put on due to the excessive amounts of sweet and fatty foods that she loved to binge on.

As she used her key card on the lock and pulled open the heavy glass door, she realized that the facility was experiencing an unusually large amount of foot traffic today, and not the kind she would have expected.

A small boy galloped past her, chasing a silver exercise ball that was nearly as tall as he was. Almost immediately there came a battle cry from the direction he was vacating, and Heidi turned to see two more boys launch into pursuit of what could only be their brother.

The resemblance between the three of them was undeniable. All three had creamy milk chocolate-colored skin and eyes that challenged the boundaries between gold and blue.

Heidi was no expert on children, but if she had to guess their ages, she would have placed them at around six or seven years old. Identical triplets, and boys to boot. She felt a swell of respect and sympathy for the mother responsible for this rambunctious litter, but it quickly warped into frustration.

Trying to get a good workout with those three little tornadoes running around was going to be impossible. She wouldn't want to risk dropping any of the weights onto a passing toe, or accidently kicking the heavy bag into the path of an unmindful runner.

She looked at the options that left for her and scowled. The pulley systems and treadmills were fine, if you were into that sort of thing, but she'd never really liked them much.

Terrific. This day just kept getting better and better. She couldn't sleep because of nightmares, and now she wouldn't get her workout either. At this rate, she would be a sleep deprived, emotional wreck by the end of the day.

"What sort of complex offers a fully equipped gym, but no daycare center?" A deep voice growled from somewhere just out of sight, and off to Heidi's left. "This is ridiculous."

Curious, she took a few steps further into the gym, guessing the source of that voice must be coming from one of the few adjacent rooms. A room that she'd never actually used before, due to her hectic schedule.

The occupied area was intended for a series of martial art classes, which were generally held in the late afternoon, while she was still at work. There was an ongoing advertisement for them at the front desk, but she'd never paid it much attention, so she wasn't sure which combative style they taught or the ages they catered to. Although she was fairly certain they weren't intended for children this young.

Then she saw him, and her train of thought crashed headlong into a sea of lust.

He was tall and broad-shouldered, but not overly wide like some of the muscle heads that frequented the gym.

Because he wasn't wearing a shirt over those body-hugging shorts, she could see that he was built hard and lean, like a panther.

He even moved like a big cat, muscles flexing and gliding beneath dark skin, as he slowly shifted his stance into a form that Heidi recognized. He was doing yoga. All alone, without a class or an instructor to guide him. And doing some pretty advanced positions too, she noted when he slowly shifted again, taking on a form that she had never mastered.

Although there was a calm balance in his expression, she could see several day's growth of stubble covering a hard jaw and firmly set lips.

He looked to be in his mid-thirties, at least a decade older than her. But lately she'd preferred a more experienced man, and she was definitely considering adding this hottie to her to-do list.

She did wish that she'd spent a little more time in front of the mirror that morning, but there was no use crying over it now. He was a gym rat, like her, and a yoga master as well. She was sure he'd seen plenty of ponytails in his lifetime, so hers wasn't likely to shock him. And if it did, then he wasn't the sort of playmate she wanted anyway.

With a happy little sway of her hips, she grinned and stepped forward to introduce herself.

The next moment she was laid out flat on the floor, blindsided by three identical steamrollers racing each other at full speed across the room.

The pain and shock of her fall, left her momentarily

paralyzed beneath a wild, thrashing tangle of angry feet and flailing arms. Several hard elbows and knees landed blows that were sure to bruise, as the boys fought to regain their footing, hollering in frustration and dismay at having their game ended in such a manner.

For one terrifying moment, her mind took her back to the vicious beatings she'd received from Craig, and she cried out in real fear. Then their diminutive figures were being lifted away and the face of her hero appeared, his golden eyes narrowed in concern.

The mysterious, and incredibly sexy, yoga master cupped her cheeks within strong, warm hands and tilted her face towards him.

"Are you alright?" He asked in a deep baritone that resonated throughout her body. "Did you hit your head? Do you feel dizzy?"

Heidi attempted a wry expression, to hide the heart-stopping effect his proximity had on her hormones. A tingling, sensual heat awakened everywhere his hands touched her. And it was being strangely amplified by the fear and adrenaline that had flooded through her system during her fall.

"I think the only thing hurt is my pride," she assured him, a bit breathlessly. "Who brings their kids to a gym anyway? Don't they have school or something?"

"School doesn't start until nine," he pointed out, helping her into a seated position.

"Yeah well, maybe I should have a talk with their mother. She shouldn't let them just run wild in here. They could get hurt or hurt someone else."

"Their mother passed away several years ago."

"How do you... oh." Heidi mentally cringed. How had she not noticed the similarities between father and sons? She sighed inwardly. Because the moment she'd laid eyes on the man, the reasonable half of her brain had shut down completely.

"I'm sorry about that," she admitted. "I should have

noticed the family resemblance. It's pretty obvious, actually."

"I usually wait until they're in school before I come down here," he assured her, also answering the unspoken question of why she'd never seen him before. "But last night was a rough one for me. I thought the gym would be fairly empty at this hour, so nobody would mind these little monsters running around."

He rolled his eyes in the direction the boys were now charging, but Heidi couldn't tear her gaze away from him.

As he talked, he delicately investigated the vertebrae in her neck and the back of her head with experienced fingertips, sending a wash of heat and pleasure shivering down through her body.

He obviously had medical training, but her regular doctor never performed physical exams while he was half naked. The temptation to stroke her hands down his beautifully sculpted chest and abs was almost overwhelming.

She wasn't used to feeling so out of control and excited at the same time. In direct contrast, everything about the man crouched over her was calm, powerful and efficient. He was a dominant and confident male. A balanced yogi. A wrangler and protector of three exuberant adolescents. And even a provider of emergency medical care for hormone blinded idiots.

His quiet, assertive manner assured her that he was the kind of guy who could take anything life threw at him in stride, and that realization gave her an unexpected thrill, unlike anything she'd ever experienced before.

"Okay, can you follow my finger using only your eyes?" He asked, at last drawing back enough to raise a hand between them.

"I don't know," she responded with her usual flippant honesty. "I'm having trouble not looking at the rest of you."

Almost immediately, she regretted the words. His dark

brows crashed together, and his eyes darkened first with confusion, and then discomfort. It was not the response she usually garnered from attractive men, which left her feeling awkward as well.

"I'm fine," she assured him quickly, rolling up onto her knees. But the moment she attempted to stand, pain lanced up her right leg.

As she crumpled back towards the floor, strong arms quickly flew up to catch her.

"Ow, I lied," she winced. "I think I twisted my ankle."

Could there be a more ridiculous injury for a girl to have? The triplets were so low to the ground, they must hit her just right, folding her ankle at the joint as she fell beneath them.

Her golden-eyed hero helped her back down into a seated position so that he could check the injured limb.

"Without an x-ray, I can't be certain," he suggested. "But I don't think it's broken. Just stay off of it as much as possible and use ice to help reduce the swelling. You'll also need to keep a wrap on it for a while and try to keep that foot elevated."

"Ugh, that's all easier said than done," she groaned. "How am I supposed to drive like this?"

"You're not," he commanded in a tone that stirred up a fresh wave of heat and excitement within her. "You either stay home or you find someone to drive you."

"I'm scheduled to work at nine, where am I going to find a ride with such short notice?" She argued, fighting her unwelcome desire to purr in submission. Until that moment, she hadn't realized how much she craved a man that could make her feel safe, while at the same time allow her to feel weak and feminine.

She'd found plenty of guys that wanted to either dominate or protect, but never one that made her feel as if he could properly balance both roles. Now, in one swift movement, the yogi of her dreams swept her up into his arms, and nearly stopped her heart.

"Boys, let's go," he called loudly, his deep voice echoing through the spacious building, effectively summoning the galloping trio to his side.

"Which floor are you on?" He asked Heidi, oblivious to the wide-eyed amazement that had all but rendered her speechless. She'd had a hard time not touching him earlier, now she was securely pressed right up against his bare chest, one open palm braced against the solid muscle directly over his heart.

The intimate proximity to his naked skin made her feel incredibly warm and sexy, lowering all of her defenses and making it difficult to remember why she had ever tried to resist him in the first place.

"I'm on thirteen."

"Lucky number thirteen," he grinned, sending her heart skipping wildly off her ribs. That smile should be registered as a deadly weapon. One more hit like that and she might stop breathing for good.

Her pulse was pounding with a wicked and unwelcome desire to slide her hand up over all that warm skin and snuggle into his embrace. But there were at least a thousand and one reasons why that was a terrible idea, and the three biggest ones were now marching along behind their father, like cheerful little doppelgangers.

She had very few rules when it came to picking out bedfellows. If they revved her engine and didn't belong to someone else, she considered them fair game. The only exception was a widowed father.

Experience had taught her that his kind really only came in two flavors.

The first group buried their hearts with their wives, which meant they were constantly comparing her to their previous love, even if they never admitted it out loud. The second group had learned to accept their loss and were now actively looking to fill the vacancy in their family.

Either way, it spelled trouble.

She needed to be the moon and stars for whomever

she was dating. She could never compete with their former wives. But at the same time, she wasn't ready to settle down yet, and she certainly wasn't ready to be a mother.

It wasn't that she didn't like kids, because she did. She even planned to have a few herself someday. But for now, she really liked her life just the way it was, without anyone to answer to but herself.

Dating daddies meant nothing but trouble, so why was she considering breaking her rule for this particularly sexy specimen?

Damn, he smelled good!

As he carried her into the elevator, she found herself embraced by the tantalizing combination of his aftershave and a hint of pure musky male. It filled the small area and made her think of all the erotic ways she could work up a good sweat with a guy like this.

"Gabe says that the number thirteen is bad luck," a small voice piped up from somewhere below Heidi, again reminding her that she was not alone with the object of her carnal obsession.

The man holding her gave a soft laugh that rumbled against her palm and made everything go all hot and gooey inside her. Oh lord! She'd already fallen half in love with his voice at the gym, but it was even deeper and sexier when he laughed.

"There's really no such thing as good luck or bad luck in a number or an object," he assured his son. "We all have the power to make our own luck, by always doing our best and being kind to others."

"Like her?"

Heidi couldn't see the boy, but she knew that she was the only female within pointing distance, and she could practically feel three small pairs of eyes staring up at her back. Then her hero was grinning down at her and she completely forgot about the boys once more. Every rational thought in her head was drowned by a flood of heat and desire.

"Yes, just like her," he rumbled softly.

A flash of warmth in his eyes warned that her current state of arousal was not entirely lost on him. Whether it was intentional or not, his arms tightened just a little around her body. It caused another tidal wave of pleasure, lust, and excitement to cascade through her system.

"Here we are, thirteenth floor," he stated cheerfully, without a hint of the desire she was certain she'd seen in him only a heartbeat earlier. Had she been wrong? Or was he disguising his interest now for the sake of his sons?

"Boys, I want you to go on up to our apartment, alright? Get ready for school. I'll be up in just a few minutes. Can you do that for me?"

They must have nodded because he smiled again. Shifting Heidi's weight slightly, he fished a key card out of his from a slim pocket in his shorts and handed it to one of them.

"Don't forget to brush your teeth," he admonished, as he stepped out of the elevator and turned to watch them go. Then the doors were closing again and he was looking down at Heidi.

"Which apartment is yours?"

"B," she answered a bit breathlessly, struggling to speak through a strange mix of fear and anticipation. In just a few steps, they would be alone together in her apartment. She wasn't entirely sure if she was strong enough to resist what her body was craving, once they were inside, and in such close proximity to her bed.

He stopped in front of her door.

"Key card?"

"It's in my back pocket."

Rather than put her down, he shifted her weight once more, pulling her up higher onto his chest. Silently forcing her to wrap her arms around his neck and hold herself up, he slid a large hand down over the curve of her bottom, and into one of the two deep pockets that decorated the rear of her sweatpants.

It wasn't until then, that she realized how thin the material actually was. A girl could feel a whole lot more through soft and pliant cotton than she might through a pair of good, solid jeans.

As his palm cupped her butt, a shock of hot pleasure exploded through her, awakening every little nerve ending in her body, and drawing a husky gasp from her lips. It was echoed by a soft rumble of sound from him.

Her face was pressed up against the side of his neck, her body crushed against his, as she felt his hand lingering, squeezing slightly as he savored the fullness of her bottom against his palm.

Then, as if realizing that he'd trespassed into very dangerous territory, he abruptly withdrew, pulling the little card from her pocket and swiping it almost savagely through the lock on her door.

Stepping inside the apartment, he hesitated for only a moment, before striding across the open floor to the bed. Without a word, he dropped her onto the mattress and stood towering over her, panting like a man finishing the last leg of a grueling marathon.

"Okay, Honey. Tell me what to bring you, so that you can get ready for work," he growled in a voice much harsher than what he'd used in the presence of his sons. "I'll place them on the bed, then I'll go get the boys and come back to pick you up."

She licked her lips, and his jaw clenched as he looked away. Why was he trying to ignore the burn between them? Was it possible he'd been out of the game for so long, he didn't see how much she wanted him?

"My name is Heidi," Her voice was hardly more than a whisper, but his gaze instantly rose to clash with hers. It scorched deeper than any flame could ever reach. Down to a part of her soul that had never been touched before.

"Did you hear what I said?" He demanded with a scowl, but there was no denying the desire blazing in those golden eyes now. They were glowing with an almost iridescent heat. It was enough to make even an experienced seductress feel like a soft, simpering little schoolgirl.

"Yes," she answered with more confidence than she felt. "But school doesn't start until nine, right?"

For a moment, he only stared down at her with those incredible eyes.

"Do you want a ride, or not?" He growled, then visibly winced. There was no denying the duality in those words.

"That's not what I meant," he snapped, as Heidi began to smile.

"I know what you meant," she assured him, pushing up off the bed to balance on her uninjured leg. "But I like the naughty implication better."

For the first time since they'd met, she saw uncertainly flicker across his face. The resulting expression was a blend of silk and steel that knocked the breath out of her lungs and set loose a million butterflies in her stomach.

She'd thought his confidence, and that powerful air of command, had been sexy as hell. But watching him now, as he struggled to retain that iron self-control, sent the most incredible thrill racing through her body. It was a heady thing to see such a magnificent male falter at the thought of being with her.

Before she could stop herself, she was reaching for him.

In a flash, he'd caught both of her wrists, preventing contact.

Unwittingly, his firm grip also awakened a surge of adrenaline that bordered upon fear. After her forced time in captivity, any sign of violence tended to stir up all of those dark and terrible memories.

The hands now holding her were firm, but surprisingly gentle. Still, she shivered as she gave a small tug and felt how securely she was contained.

Wide eyes flashed quickly up to meet his, and she knew he could see everything that she was feeling written stark and raw upon her face. It was clear in the way that his expression darkened and the muscles in his jaw tensed.

His hands fell away, freeing her. But Heidi felt only a rise of anger and frustration at the release, rather than relief. She didn't want him to see her as weak or damaged, so instead of retreating from him, she pushed forward.

With only one supporting leg, she might have fallen to her knees if he'd chosen to step backward and avoid the connection. But he didn't. As her open palms struck his chest, he merely spread his arms, and closed them again around her.

Somehow that shocked her more than a fall.

He pulled her tight against his body, letting her feel every single hard muscle down his entire length. Then he looked at her with a long, hard stare that both terrified and aroused.

"I'm not the man you're looking for," he stated, in a low, threatening tone.

"Yes, you are," she challenged, reaching up to tangle her arms around his neck. But there was a slight trembling in her limbs now, and she knew he felt it.

Abruptly, one of his hands was fisted in her hair, and Heidi's lips parted on a breathless gasp. There was no pain, but there was also no escape.

Tilting her head up, he forced her to meet his gaze. His other arm tightened around her waist, pulling her up onto her toes. Despite his greater height, their lips were now only a whisper apart. If he dipped his head, even a fraction, their lips would touch.

She could feel the warmth of his breath feathering over her mouth, and her whole body vibrated beneath the sensation.

"It will never happen," he growled so softly that she felt, rather than heard the words. Then he took one sharp stride forward and deposited her back upon the bed.

Ignoring her small cry of surprise, he turned and stepped briskly over to the dresses hanging up between her wardrobes. He shuffled quickly through the collection, before tossing one onto the bed beside her.

"Business length, but with a sexy cut. That strikes me as the sort of thing you'd probably wear," he stated simply. "I'll go pick up the boys and come back for you."

Heidi was staring at him, slack jawed, but as he turned away again, she managed to find her voice.

"I'll be calling in sick today. Don't bother coming back. Ever."

CHAPTER TWO

Her boss was less than thrilled to hear that Heidi was injured, but tax season was over and he could afford to be generous with the schedule.

"Go ahead and take a couple weeks off," he grumbled. "But I'll see you back in the office bright and early on the first. In a wheelchair, if necessary. You know I can't survive very long without you."

"I'm only a phone call away," she reminded him.

"That's not the same," he argued. "The office feels too drab and quiet without you flouncing around."

"I have never flounced a day in my life," she laughed, feeling some of her good humor returning. Her mysterious yoga master, slash hero, had really done a number on her self-confidence.

After saying goodbye, she dropped the little cell phone onto the bed and scowled down at the purple bruise beginning to discolor the skin around her ankle. She'd never have been injured if she hadn't been so focused on flirting.

Her mind rebelliously summoned up a perfect memory of his half-naked body, flexing and gliding from one difficult yoga form to the next. Immediately, she felt a fluttery wash of excitement in her tummy, which really pissed her off.

She was a strong and fiercely independent woman. She didn't need a man complicating her life this way. There were hundreds, even thousands of men out there, most of which would be more than happy to warm her bed, without half of the stress.

So what if she was going through a dry spell right now. Craig's brutality had made it hard for her to trust anyone enough to let them get very close. Even her yogi master had elicited a fear response when he'd grabbed her.

She sighed.

But she didn't want anyone else. She wanted him. A man whose name she didn't even know. A man with three young boys, and the goddess only knew what kind of post-widowhood issues.

It wasn't just because he'd looked incredibly edible in those skintight gym shorts either. Sexy guys were a dime a dozen. She had a little black phonebook full of numbers she'd collected over the years.

This particular man had a presence about him. Something she couldn't really define, but it set him apart from all the others. His strength, his manner, even the way that he moved, spoke of quiet power and control.

He was a man that would almost certainly instill a sense of respect and admiration in others. But at the same time, she'd seen a gentleness and good humor in him as he'd interacted with his sons.

Of all the men that had marched in and out of her life over the years, maybe that was the reason she was crushing so hard over a single dad. Maybe, after all of the pain and the fear that Craig had awakened in her life, she needed a man that could both take charge and protect, as well as soothe and seduce.

She touched her lips with trembling fingertips. A shiver of pleasure tickled down her spine as she recalled the heat of his breath there. It didn't matter that she didn't know his name, or that he had kids, or that he'd forcefully rejected her after making her so hot she thought she might spontaneously combust.

He'd wanted her as much as she'd wanted him. But he'd denied her.

"Damn it!" She snarled, picking the phone back up and clicking a number on her speed dial.

The best way to get over a guy, was to get under a new one. She just needed to rustle up some female supporters and have one of them drive her down to the medical clinic for a quick exam and an ankle brace. Then she'd start working her way through some of those phone numbers in her little black book. There had to be at least one potential date in a pool of that size.

It was time to break this sexual drought, before she did something really stupid, like fell head over heels in love with a father of triplets.

* * *

By six o'clock that evening, she was looking as sexy as a girl could manage, while wearing a hideous black brace that covered the lower half of her leg. She'd have taken it off and left it at home, but she couldn't really walk without it, and Morgan would have refused to drive her to the nightclub.

"This is ridiculous," Morgan suggested for at least the tenth time since they'd left Heidi's apartment and headed into the town for an impromptu girls night out. "You should be sitting on the couch at home, with your leg elevated and a bag of frozen peas on your ankle."

"Is Rachel planning on making an appearance? Or is she still in New York with her sexy billionaire?" Heidi asked, once again changing the subject. It was scary enough to be facing the dating world once more. She didn't need her friend making things worse.

"She and Tyson got home late this afternoon," Morgan

scowled, obviously aware of Heidi's attempts to distract her. "I believe they're planning a quiet evening alone. You know how much she hates the big city."

Heidi sighed.

"I can't possibly imagine why. If it wasn't for my absolute devotion to the two of you, I'd have moved there years ago. Maybe I'll go after you're both married, with little rugrats hanging off your shirttails." She cut suspicious eyes towards her friend. "Leo hasn't proposed yet has he? You know that I better be the first person you call or I'll never speak to you again."

Morgan's cheeks colored as Heidi had known they would. The girl could be adorably shy about her relationship.

"You and Rachel are the closest thing I have to family," Morgan pointed out with a demure shrug. "Who else would I call? Speaking of which, are you going to tell me why you really called tonight? What is the real reason we are going to the club, when you should be at home resting your ankle?"

Heidi scowled, as a fresh surge of frustration and desire flooded her system. Just thinking of the mysterious yogi made her squirm a little in her seat. Unfortunately, Morgan knew her well enough to guess the answer.

"This is about a guy, isn't it," the girl guessed correctly. "So what did he do? Did he cheat on you or something?"

Heidi snorted.

"It's hard to cheat on someone that you refuse to even kiss."

Morgan feigned horror.

"Someone actually turned you down? What's wrong with him? Is he married?"

"Not anymore," Heidi shook her head, trying not to hear the poorly disguised amusement in her friend's voice. "He's gorgeous, athletic, smells incredible, and has a voice that could melt the panties off a nun."

"I can't imagine why someone like that wouldn't kill for

a taste of your lips." Morgan tried to sound shocked, but Heidi could see the laughter bubbling up behind her eyes. Both Rachel and Morgan had long teased her about her trouble with men.

Before Craig, Heidi tended to love them and leave them with almost supernatural speed. Now however… she cringed inwardly, not wanting to admit just how dismal her love life had become.

Her friends had often warned that she would eventually find a man that could turn the game around and leave her feeling like a dog chasing her tail. From the look on her face, Morgan obviously thought that the fateful meeting had at last occurred.

Heidi frowned. Maybe it had.

"Oh he wanted a taste," she growled, trying to assure herself that what she'd seen in his eyes had been real. "I was right there, just inches from his mouth, and he looked like he was going to bust something he wanted it so bad. Then he just shoved me away, like I was an obnoxious cat."

Morgan's eyes abruptly widened at those last words. A sharp look of real concern, almost fear, flickering across her face. But Heidi continued, her scowl deepening as she considered the biggest reason she needed to forget all about her sexy hero.

"He's a single dad. With triplets. Boys. Little hyperactive ones."

Morgan's surprise was genuine, the concern in her face deepening.

"Are you serious? Wow! I thought you didn't date dads."

"I don't. I'm not dating him. He just…he sort of…rescued me, kind of. He carried me up to my apartment after his boys ran me over," she finished lamely.

"Heidi, I don't think we should go to the club tonight…"

"Don't you dare back out on me," Heidi yelped. "You

don't have any idea how messed up my head is right now. I need this! I can't stop thinking about him."

Morgan winced and looked strangely guilty.

"I think there's something I should tell you," her friend started, but Heidi gave her a look of pure desperation that shut her up.

"Please don't ask me not to go tonight. You know that I would never be seen in public with this horrible cast if the situation wasn't dire," Heidi pointed out with brutal honesty. "But I know it has a lot to do with the dry spell I'm in right now. I just need one night with a great guy and I'll forget all about the daddy issue."

Morgan didn't look convinced, but she didn't put up any further argument.

CHAPTER THREE

"Your place or mine?"

The man who'd introduced himself as Gary, flashed her a perfect smile as he deposited his empty glass onto a nearby table and slid one possessive arm around Heidi's waist.

She wasn't usually interested in men who wore business suits and ties to a night club, but there weren't a lot of good prospects here tonight, and her attempts to reach any of the numbers in her phone book had flopped.

Most decent guys just weren't able to pull off an impromptu date in the middle of the week. Which left her attempting to pick up one of the not-so-decent losers currently hanging out at the bar.

At least this guy didn't talk like a suit, and she'd caught sight of a tattoo on his forearm when he'd paid for their drinks.

She usually liked her guys intelligent, at least moderately successful, clean and respectful, but with a few rough edges. Someone that could get down and dirty with her in the bedroom but cleaned up pretty for Sunday dinner.

Gary was not someone she would have picked under usual circumstances, but she just couldn't go home alone, not tonight. This was emergency therapy. If she didn't break this self-inflicted dry spell, she just knew she'd be knocking on a certain yoga master's door in the near future, swallowing all of her pride and begging for something that she'd never had to ask twice for in her life.

"Yours," she finally agreed. As much as she wanted this to work out, she wasn't about to have him invade her sanctuary. "Let me go get my coat and let my ride know she can go on home without me. I'll meet you at the front door."

Morgan was sitting at the bar talking to Mike, the bartender.

Mike had gone to high school with the girls, and even had a brief fling with Heidi one summer. They'd all stayed friends and still enjoyed each other's company, when their busy schedules allowed.

For a minute, Heidi considered canceling her plans with Gary and just asking Mike to come home with her instead. But the man was working. His shift wouldn't end until three or four in the morning, and she didn't think she could wait that long. If she delayed, she would almost certainly reconsider what she was doing. Then she'd absolutely be going home alone.

With every hour that passed, she found her thoughts dwelling more and more upon the one man that she absolutely did not want to think about.

"Hey Morgan," she tried to look happy as she collected her coat and purse from the adjoining barstool. "It looks like I'm going home with the suit standing next to the front door. Gary something-or-other. I'll call you in the morning, okay?"

"Are you sure?" Morgan was wearing that worried, guilty look again.

"Yes," Heidi hugged her. "I'll be fine. You'll see. This is just what the doctor ordered."

Going home with her last chance date did actually feel like something she was being prescribed, rather than something she wanted, but she wasn't about to admit that to Morgan.

As she sat in the passenger seat of his car and only half listened to him taking about the funeral he'd come into town to attend, Heidi began to seriously regret her stubborn nature. Her date was rapidly losing his charm and she was not about to sleep with someone that didn't at least interest her a little.

Not even in a desperate attempt to forget about hard muscles flexing and releasing, carrying a perfectly sculpted body through an admirable list of yoga poses. Or to stop thinking about how flexible her limber hero might have been in bed.

Her pulse spiked as she recalled the heat and strength of his bare chest beneath her palm, and the blaze of desire that had leapt into his golden eyes.

She recalled how his hands had shook, as he held her pinned fiercely to his body, his lips hovering just above hers. He had almost lost control. Almost.

If she had touched him then, even a stroke of her fingertips against his flesh, she was sure that he would have combusted. All of that carefully controlled lust would have surged up to take control and burn them both to the ground.

There was no doubt about it, a man like that would take everything she had to give, and he'd still demand more. He'd held almost a supernatural command over her body.

Even if he hadn't held her so fiercely, she would have felt it.

She swallowed a muffled whimper as her wretched imagination summoned up all of her darkest and most secret fantasies. Things that she'd never been brave enough to try with anyone else.

Was it possible that she had finally found a man capable of fulfilling those cravings?

If so, what the heck was she doing, going home with

this moronic poser?

"Stop, wait, please," she gasped, interrupting his mundane prattle about a rude airline stewardess. "I've changed my mind. I'm sorry. Could you please take me home?"

For a minute he looked confused, then he shrugged.

"Okay, I guess."

Within a few minutes, she was relieved to be pulling into her apartment building's underground lot. It was the first thing all night that actually felt right.

Gary helped her out of the car, and Heidi again silently cursed the ugly black boot on her ankle.

"Thank you for understanding," she smiled apologetically. "I'm just really not in the mood anymore. It's been a rough week for me, as you've probably already guessed."

She gestured towards her injured limb and gave a small laugh, but he didn't look amused.

In fact, he looked angry.

"What are talking about? I thought we were going up to your place. You sound like you're trying to brush me off."

Heidi frowned and shook her head.

"I told you in the car, I've changed my mind. I'm sorry, but I'm just not feeling up for anything more tonight."

"You told me you changed your mind about going to my place. You never said that the night was going to end the minute we showed up here. You can't just let a guy down like that. Besides, judging from the way you were dancing with me tonight, I don't think that ankle is going to slow you down much. Especially after I have you horizontal," he pointed out, apparently trying to reason with her.

Then he destroyed whatever sympathy she might have felt for him.

"Just give me fifteen minutes. I'll be quick."

Heidi snorted in disgust.

"If you meant for that to sound seductive, you failed. I

said no, and I mean it."

Rage darkened his eyes and brought a twist of fear to her gut.

She wasn't sure if she stood her ground because she wanted him to see that she was serious, or because she was suddenly so scared she couldn't move. A horror reel of memories, all featuring Craig's attack on her, had begun playing through her mind.

The date had just gone from bad, to apocalyptic.

With her ankle in a medical boot, there was no possible way she was going to outrun this guy, even if he'd given her a chance. Which he didn't. Instead, he seized her upper arms and began to shove her back around towards the car.

"You've been begging for this all night," he snarled in a voice that now terrified her. "If you don't want to go upstairs, fine. But we will be having sex. You owe me that much."

"No!" Heidi screamed, kicking out at her attacker without thinking.

The heavy brace caught him right in the shin, making them both howl in pain.

He reared up like a rabid bear, one fisted hand aimed at her head. But the blow never landed. Instead, she was treated to the sight of his nose blossoming into a red stain on his face.

"She said no," a deep voice explained, almost matter-of-factly. It was followed by a second blow. Which crumpled her attacker onto the pavement beside his car, and left him clutching his stomach, wheezing for air.

A powerful body abruptly moved between Heidi and the fallen man, shielding her from his view.

"Are you alright?" That incredible voice asked her, and for the second time in as many days, Heidi found herself looking up into the golden eyes of an unexpected hero.

Her body instantly came alive with excitement and desire, washing away any of the fear which might have lingered.

She knew that he'd asked her a question, but she found it impossible to speak.

He was here. Her hero. He had saved her. Again.

When she didn't immediately answer, he muttered a furious curse for the failed rapist who was attempting to crawl around the car to the driver's door. It looked as though he'd like to follow the man and add a few well-placed kicks.

But he remained by Heidi's side, his golden eyes softening with sympathy as he held out one hand towards her, the palm facing up.

"I know you probably don't want to be touched right now, but may I at least walk you back to your apartment?"

It didn't take much effort for her to stand, even with the awkward boot. He practically lifted her onto her feet and continued to hold her hand so she could steady herself. But that was impossible while she was this close to him.

Everything inside her was crying out to be closer, and she just wasn't prepared to fight that attraction right now. She shocked them both by abruptly throwing herself into his arms and burying her face beneath his chin.

Powerful arms immediately closed around her, pressing her tight to his chest.

It felt so good to be in his arms again, like coming home after a long, hard journey. But there was also something more. A deep hungry need that flooded through her system and sent her heart skipping around her ribs.

"Thank you," she whispered against his throat, and felt a soft sigh of understanding rumble up from deep within him.

"We should get you upstairs," he suggested in a gentle tone, as large hands slowly pushed her away.

Gary had finally made it back into his car and the engine abruptly roared to life, snarling and spitting as the man behind the wheel gave it too much gas in his hurry to vacate the premises.

With one wary eye on the retreating vehicle, Heidi allowed herself to be pulled up onto the walkway and out of harm's way.

"How did you know?" She murmured, as her hero escorted her onto the elevator and waited until the doors were safely closed behind them, blocking out all sight and sound of her attacker and his escape. "How did you know that I needed you?"

She watched her companion, as the muscles in his jaw tightened and his expression darkened.

"I didn't," he growled softly. "I had just finished my workout at the gym and was heading back upstairs."

Was that a spark of fear in his eyes? She looked again, but it was gone. She must have been mistaken. What could a man like this possibly be afraid of?

"Who the hell was that guy anyway?" He demanded. "Please tell me that he isn't your boyfriend. You don't deserve to be treated like that. By anyone. They have groups for women..."

"He's not my boyfriend," she hurried to interrupt. "He was just a really bad choice that I'm glad to be rid of."

He looked relieved. Maybe more relieved than a simple do-gooder had a right to be. Was he simply expressing the self-righteous anger that any red-blooded male would possess against someone capable of violently harming a helpless woman? Or was it possible that he'd felt a touch of jealousy when he'd seen her with another man?

She tried not to feel happy about that second possibility, but it was hard. There was nothing she wanted more than to be held by him again. Or better yet, to feel his lips pressed against hers.

A firestorm of lust raced through her veins as she stole a glance up from beneath her lashes and caught his gaze traveling down over her body. This time there was no mistaking the sexual interest in his eyes.

It was enough to make her limbs feel weak and caused

a tight ball of nervous excitement to awaken in her stomach. He definitely wanted her. His eyes were practically eating her up, caressing every curve and plane with such intensity, it scorched her flesh and left a brand deep upon her soul.

No man had ever looked at her this way. As if he would gladly have given his life just to touch her.

Before that moment, she would have denied the possibility of predestined love. But how else could she explain looking into a stranger's face and feeling as if there was something unseen and magically which connected him to you?

Golden eyes flashed up to meet hers and she could see the barely restrained, primal hunger burning there. The very same undeniable need, wrapped in confusion, which was threatening to drown her.

"You feel it too. Don't you?" She spoke in only a whisper, as if afraid that words might somehow break the spell. "There's something happening between us. Something that makes me crave your touch more than I crave my next breath."

The air escaped through his fiercely clenched teeth, sounding almost like a snarl of anger. His hands were now curled into white-knuckled fists at his side, and his whole body was tense, every muscle in sharp outline.

"You don't even know my name," he growled. "You're just shook up by what happened with that asshole in the parking lot. You'll feel better after you get some sleep."

Heidi frowned. He didn't have to be so prickly. She wasn't exactly thrilled about the way she felt either. He was a single dad, the very last person she'd ever have chosen to feel this strongly about.

But she wouldn't – couldn't – deny her attraction.

"So?" She asked simply. "Tell me your name."

His gaze flashed to the little glowing numbers on the elevator panel, as if silently wishing they would speed up and end his torment.

Heidi just waited, until at last he sighed.

"Jerome."

The name sounded strangely familiar and right to her. She repeated it out loud, feeling a small shiver trickle down her spine as the syllables slid over her tongue.

Beside her, he made a low harsh sound, as if hearing her speak his name caused him physical pain.

"As I've already told you, my name is Heidi," she offered in return. "I don't date single dads."

He gave a harsh laugh.

"That wouldn't stop me from throwing you down on that big bed of yours, and making you forget everything but the sound of my name on your lips, and the command of my body over yours."

The breath caught in her lungs as she was suddenly teetering on legs that were no longer steady enough to carry her.

Yes! Oh please, yes! Her body was instantly begging for him to make good on that threat. Every cell, every nerve, seared by the erotic image he'd just created in her mind.

His eyes blazed as he watched her lips part on a silent moan, her expression growing soft and full of undisguised desire. It seemed to pull him inevitably forward, despite the hard scowl darkening his features and the rigid tension in his body.

She was both frightened and excited by the savage challenge in his approach, slowly backing away, as hot shivers of pleasure feathered down her spine. When the cold, hard metal of the elevator doors connected with her back, she nearly moaned with anticipation.

There was nowhere left to run.

He took one more step, letting her feel the heat of his breath upon her skin, but nothing more. He kept only a heartbeat of space between them, but it couldn't stop her from basking in the warmth of his proximity.

"Stop looking at me as if I'm some kind of hero," his breath snarled against her cheek. "Just because you know my name, doesn't mean you know who I am. I'm not the kind of guy you're looking for."

She lifted her chin to meet his gaze, shivering again as she was scorched by the heat she found there.

"You don't know me. So how do you know what I'm looking for?"

He gave a soft chuckle that made everything inside her melt. If he did that again, she was pretty sure she'd be begging to bear his future children. Then he breached the gap between them, and she could think of nothing but the heat of his fingertips against her jaw, tilting her face up just the smallest fraction.

His mouth lightly brushed over hers, scarcely touching, as if fearful of what it might bring. And he was right to be afraid. The moment their lips touched, that hot electrical attraction between them blazed into something neither could have predicted.

It was a ravenous, devouring need that transcended anything a simple mortal might ever experience. This was a supernatural force, which had Jerome's surging forward, his body fiercely pinning hers against the unforgiving metal of the elevator doors.

His hands were fisted to either side of her face, pressed against the hard steel as if his life depended upon it. Because, if he allowed himself to hold her now, he would never be able to let her go.

Then the doors were opening, and he barked a curse as he grabbed Heidi to keep her from falling out onto her ass.

The moment she was steady on her feet, he released her again, dropping fisted hands to his sides.

"Go home," He snapped. "And pray you don't see me again."

"No," she shot back. But it was more of a knee-jerk response than a refusal. She was fighting so hard to cut through the confusion and desire that was fogging up her thoughts, she would have argued anything that came out of his mouth.

He stepped forward, and she stepped back. He took another step, and she retreated again.

A flash of triumph sparked in his eyes as the elevator doors began to close again... between them. She'd been so blinded to everything else, she hadn't even realized that he'd chased her out, until it was too late.

But this was what she wanted right? She didn't want to be with a single dad.

Except, she did. She wanted it more than she'd ever wanted anything in her life.

🐈 CHAPTER FOUR

Who the hell did Jerome think he was anyway?

Heidi was pacing across her apartment floor, silently raging. She'd showered and changed into comfortable sweats and a t-shirt, but she was still steaming.

The man was a single dad with three extremely hyper little boys. Dates couldn't be easy for him to get. Which meant his sex life must be worse than a nun's. So why was he turning her down?

She was a highly desirable woman, with some pretty incredible bedroom skills, if her past conquests were to be believed. She would have been the best thing that ever happened to that golden-eyed bastard.

The more she thought about it, the angrier she got. She wasn't going to be happy now until she could understand exactly why he was refusing her. And it better be good. She'd never backed down from such a challenge in her life.

Hobbling out to the elevator in the awkward ankle brace took a little of the steam out of her step. It was hard to feel powerful and commanding when you were wearing a hideous black boot strapped to half your leg. But she was too mad to stop now.

It wasn't until she was actually riding up in the elevator,

that she realized she hadn't the faintest clue which apartment was his.

She knew it had to be on one of the two floors above hers, but there were at least half a dozen suites on each floor. Her only option would be to knock on doors and hope that Jerome eventually opened one of them. With an injured ankle and two floors to cover, that plan would never work.

Her best chance of finding him again would be to stake out the gym tomorrow. A man with his mastery of yoga probably stuck to a schedule, even if it was occasionally upset by his role as a single father.

The elevator doors opened, but she didn't get off. Instead, she pushed the button to take her back down to her own floor. Yet just as the doors began to close, a familiar figure darted past, chasing two wild-eyed kittens.

With that dark complexion and those beautiful golden eyes, there was no mistaking the boy's relationship to the man Heidi was seeking.

Quickly thrusting her hands forward to stop the closing doors, she limped out into the hallway, following the racing child as fast as her booted ankle would allow.

"Hey kid, wait up!" She called as he reached the far corner and was about to vanish from view.

The boy threw a glance back at her from over his shoulder, but he didn't slow down one iota.

At the speed those kittens had been moving, they'd probably lead the boy all the way back around to lap her in another minute or two. But she kept moving doggedly forward, hoping to catch a glimpse of the boy again as she reached the corner where he'd vanished.

Instead, she was greeted by all three of the triplets standing side by side, like a particularly disturbing reenactment of a scene from The Shining.

"Uh, hi guys," she swallowed uncomfortably. How exactly did someone ask a child where they lived, without sounding like a creeper?

She really needed to brush up on child etiquette. Rachel might know what the rules were in a situation like this, but Heidi was forced to wing it.

"Is your dad around? I need to talk to him."

"He's in our apartment," one of the boys answered, with a nod towards a door marked as suite C.

"Thanks," she smiled, feeling as if the brief exchange had been a smashing success. Then the boys abruptly stampeded through the door, before she could knock, leaving it wide open as they began calling for their father.

"Dad, the nanny is here!"

Nanny? Wrong! Heidi hesitated for only a minute. The boys hadn't technically invited her inside. But they'd left the door wide open, and it felt rather ridiculous standing in the hall while she was being hugely misrepresented to the man she'd come here to seduce.

"Nope! Not the nanny," she called, stepping just onto the threshold, but her voice was drowned out by the yowling trio.

How was it possible that she didn't hear them stampeding around like this through her ceiling? She really had to hand it to the company that had built this complex. They'd done a kick ass job of insulating and soundproofing the place.

She suspected Tyson Asgard might have had a hand in it. Rachel's billionaire boyfriend had the Midas touch when it came to real estate development. His properties were expensive, but always very well built.

A deep voice cut through her silent musings and drew her gaze to the man emerging from a corner room.

"Dad, Dad, the nanny is here."

Despite her loud protest, the boys were insistent.

She was more than a little irritated by the mistake, until Jerome looked up, and she saw the dark emotions brewing in his eyes. She was very clearly the last person that he wanted to see standing in his living room.

"You're not the nanny," he growled, as if she were

guilty of some kind of deception.

"No kidding," she returned, with just as much growl in her voice. "But they apparently take after their dad and were born deaf to whatever I have to say."

Before he could respond, the boys returned to the room lugging a massive suitcase between them.

"Here you go, Dad. We've got your bag for you. Now you won't miss your plane."

Heidi's eyebrows crashed together in understanding.

"You're leaving," she stated the obvious.

He cast a frustrated scowl towards the clock, then sighed.

"Not if the real nanny doesn't get here in the next thirty seconds. The taxi driver has been waiting for so long, I'll probably owe him a kidney."

Abruptly, he straightened, and gave Heidi a look that should have sent her scurrying off in the other direction. But masochistic curiosity kept her rooted to her place for thirty seconds too long.

"Could you watch the boys for me? Just until the nanny shows up. You do owe me a favor," he added when he saw her gearing up for a loud refusal. "Please."

Heidi's mouth had opened, but the words, 'not a chance in hell', got caught on the guilty hook in her throat.

"I don't know anything about taking care of kids," she told him, but her horrified gaze was now focused on the trio of identical adolescents, which had burst into cheers at their father's suggestion.

No doubt they thought she looked as gullible as a guppy chasing dust motes.

"Besides, you hardly know me," she argued. "I could be a serial killer."

All three boys fell temporarily silent, looking even more fascinated and excited than before. Heidi rolled her eyes back towards their father, desperately clinging to the hope that she could change his mind.

"The management here does exceptional background

checks of all their tenants," he pointed out, grabbing the handle of his suitcase and easily hefting it up out of the boys' grasp. "Besides, their usual nanny should arrive shortly. I think the boys will survive that long."

"Yeah, maybe. But how do I survive them?" She panicked as he strode past her, heading for the elevator. "Seriously, I don't know anything about kids!"

"Just put a movie on and wait for the nanny," he suggested. "You'll be fine."

Then the elevator doors were closing, and Heidi found herself turning to see three pairs of curious little eyes staring up at her.

Oh, sweet goddess, she was doomed!

"Can we watch Killer Robots?" One of the boys piped up. "It's super scary. The robots go crazy and cut everybody up."

"Ew. No." Heidi frowned. "Why don't you turn on Bambi, or something like that?"

"That's a baby movie!" They began protesting.

"I want something scary..."

"Something with robots..."

"No, something with monsters..."

"No, robots!"

"Monsters!"

"Shush!" Heidi snapped, loudly enough to silence all three in amazement. "Just turn on the cartoon channel or something. I need to make a phone call."

The boys stampeded towards the TV with such excitement, she suspected the cartoon channel was not often given to them as an option. But she only needed to keep them occupied until the tardy nanny arrived, then she could go home and leave the hired help to deny them their fun.

She'd claimed she needed to make a phone call, but as she stared at the numbers on the screen, she realized there was really no point. Nobody could rescue her from this situation. She didn't have Jerome's contact information, and she had no idea which nanny service he used.

Shoving the phone back into her pocket, she closed the gaping front door and took a few minutes to collect herself.

This apartment was much larger than hers, but it felt smaller because of the interior walls. The square footage was broken down into three bedrooms, two bathrooms, a living room, and a kitchen with a dining area.

Feeling a little guilty, she nevertheless allowed her curiosity to lead her into the master bedroom. It had minimal decorations, with a heavy king-sized bed placed in a focal position.

A desk and several bookshelves made up the rest of the space.

On the desk were several neat stacks of papers and folders, but nothing that held much interest for her. Most of them were bills, notices from the school the boys attended, or drawings and report cards tracking their development.

The desk drawers were locked, which piqued her interest, but she suspected they held nothing more than financial information and other sensitive material. The real treasures were uncovered in the accent tables which stood to either side of the massive bed.

So, he was not the abstinence practicing monk that he would have had her believe. With a pleased smile, she closed the drawer and let her fingertips play along the surface of his mattress.

She could smell the faint scent of his shampoo, and the richer tones of his natural musk, still clinging to the fabric.

This was Jerome's private sanctuary. This was where he kept his secrets, and where she had half hoped this evening would find her. Wrapped within his arms, at last given a taste of what he'd been denying her.

Well, she was here now, and he was miles away on a flight to who knows where. Doing who knows what... or whom.

She gave a soft snarl of frustration and left his room behind. There was no use driving herself crazy over 'what-ifs' and 'what-might-have-been'.

Just down the hall was the boys' room. There was no mistaking the chaos within for anything else. But it was obvious that that apartment designers had intended this to be the master suite, because it was nearly twice the size of Jerome's room.

In one corner was a cleverly designed triple bunk bed, with built in drawers and shelf space. The second corner was an indoor, wooden jungle gym, complete with a rope ladder, climbing wall, elevated club house, and a slide.

But the third corner was dedicated to Cat Heaven. What else would you call those enormous towers? Complete with ropes, ramps, tunnels, nets, and an unfathomable collection of bells and dangles of every description.

She recalled the two kittens she'd seen one of the boys chasing out in the foyer, but there was no sign of the creatures now.

With such a palatial home, she wondered how often they actually made contact with their human caretakers. She was certain they could probably loose themselves for days within those carpet covered towers.

She wasn't much of a cat person, so she didn't bother attempting to look for them. Instead, she explored the last of the bedrooms, which was smaller than the first two and probably intended as a nursery or occasional guest room. It was furnished with only a queen-sized bed, a dresser, a simple desk and a small entertainment system.

It looked almost too sterile, like a hotel room. Heidi suspected this was where the nanny slept when she was asked to watch the boys overnight.

Speaking of which, Heidi checked her watch. It was nearly nine thirty, a full hour since Jerome had promised her that the nanny would arrive. One entire hour since he had performed his vanishing act and left her with three children which she had no idea how to care for.

Surely the boys would need to go to bed soon. Tomorrow was a school day, wasn't it? Didn't schools accept the same prescribed holidays that government officers followed? Damn that man's sexy hide, he hadn't even given her the hint of a schedule for...

Oh, sweet goddess, she didn't even know their names!

What the hell was she still doing here? Maybe she should just call child welfare and have them send someone out to take this problem off her hands.

As she walked back into the living room, she realized that such drastic actions would be unnecessary, all three boys were sprawled across the couch and floor, fast asleep.

The TV continued to drone on in the background, as Heidi somehow managed to drag each little boy - one by one - up into her arms, then limp and clunk her way down the hall to their bedroom.

There was no way for her to guess which bed belonged to which boy, so she simply started at the top and worked her way down. They'd have to sleep in their clothes tonight, but she did remove their socks and shoes, leaving them in a pile on the floor.

Before turning out the light, she couldn't help but smile a bit. She liked them much better when they were sleeping. They were almost cherubic, with long lashes settled against pink cheeks, and only the occasional twitch of a toe or a nose as they dreamed.

Too bad they weren't this quiet during the day.

Heading back down the hall and into the living room, she switched the channel on the television to a crime drama and crashed down onto the couch. Where the heck was that nanny? Had there been an accident? Was the woman lying in a ditch somewhere, praying for rescue?

An evil part of Heidi almost hoped so, because the alternative was that the wench had simply left Jerome high and dry. Which meant that nobody would be coming to save Heidi before the boys woke up in the morning.

Good goddess! What was she supposed to do if that happened?

Attempting to outmaneuver a tidal wave of panic, she quickly lurched to her feet and went to raid the kitchen.

Within an hour, she was feeling almost smug, swallowing the last glass of the moderately expensive bottle of wine she'd found.

She chased the lovely merlot down with a plate full of Oreo cookies.

It made her feel almost naughty to be combining items from such opposite ends of extravagance, especially when both items were stolen from the pantry of a man she now held a rather large grudge against.

A grudge, and a crush, she silently corrected. Because she hadn't managed to stop thinking about him all night.

Her TV show ended, and Heidi stifled a massive yawn. It was getting late, even for her. It was also painfully obvious that the nanny was either lost or not coming at all. There was no use waiting up for her any longer.

Standing, Heidi felt the world buck and whirl beneath her feet, forcing her to collapse back down onto the couch and grip her spinning head between her palms.

Ugh. Her excessive consumption of sugar and alcohol had turned her sense of balance into a lopsided merry-go-round, with a psychotic clown conductor.

Wincing, she used the remote to turn off the TV, then carefully eased herself back up into a semi-hunched position.

There was no possible way she was going to make it all the way down the hall to the nanny's room. But why should she even try? Jerome's bed was much larger, and it had looked much more comfortable.

Besides, it wasn't as if he would be using it.

If he dared to complain about a drunk woman crashing in his room, she'd be happy to point out all of the ways that he could go screw himself for abandoning her to get his three boys ready for school in the morning… with a hangover. She was pretty sure she'd be regretting that wine in the morning.

Stripping down to her t-shirt and underwear, she crawled under the soft Egyptian cotton sheets, and purred at the way Jerome's scent wafted up to embrace her. Oh my, she was going to have some pleasant dreams tonight.

Maybe it was the alcohol talking, but snuggling into his bed - without his permission, and without his knowledge - was almost an erotic experience.

A wicked little smile curled the corners of her mouth as she drifted off to sleep.

🐈 CHAPTER FIVE

A feathery caress of fingertips traced down her side and lingered at the curve of her hip. Heidi sighed and snuggled closer to the heat against her back. If this was a wine-induced dream, she knew who her subconscious must have summoned.

"Bastard," she growled, and felt the body behind her tense.

"I'm sorry," Jerome's deep voice murmured against the curve of her neck.

"The nanny never showed up."

"I noticed."

"You abandoned me with three kids that don't even know my name," she pointed out, scowling into the darkness.

"They know your name," he assured her, then he threw a curve ball. "I've talked to them about you."

"Really, why?" She was honestly surprised, as she'd only seen the boys once before tonight. The day they had trampled her in the gym, while she was drooling over their father.

If she'd made any impression on them, it was probably bad.

"I wanted to know how they would feel if I started dating you," he offered simply, but there was an edge to his voice now that hadn't been there before. "Those boys mean everything to me."

"They should," she offered a slight shrug. "You're their father."

Which was also the reason Heidi should now be shoving off to go spend the rest of the night in the nanny's room. But it just felt too damned nice to be held by him this way. She'd always been a sucker for a guy that liked to cuddle.

"I don't date single dads," she reminded him.

"Then why are you in my bed?"

She fell silent, because she really wasn't sure. From the moment she'd first laid eyes on him, she'd wanted a taste of this man. Now, here she was, lying in his arms, and realizing it wasn't enough.

He fascinated her on a level she'd never prepared for. She didn't just want one passionate night with him. She needed to discover whatever it was about him that made her feel this way. The reason why she was even willing to accept his children, just to be close to him.

She rolled over to confront the enigmatic man at her back, and her legs tangled in his. With a flush of heat, she realized he wasn't wearing pajamas. In fact, he wasn't wearing anything at all.

"You're naked," she pointed out, a bit nervously, and felt the soft vibration of his laughter against her palms.

"I always sleep naked," he rumbled in a voice that had grown dangerously deep and seductive. "Is that a deal breaker for you?"

A shivery wash of pleasure raced through her body, forming a pool of heat in areas best not spoken of in polite conversation.

"I don't mind, so long as you give me the same freedoms," She laughed softly. "And if you'll promise to lock the bedroom door. I would rather not have your boys privy to our sleeping arrangement."

He chuckled again.

"Agreed. Now, shall we discuss your punishment for drinking all of my wine?"

Her breath caught in her throat, and her heart began to race, as a hot burst of excitement shot through her body. He must have felt her trembling, because he pulled her tighter to his chest and held her there with firm, protective arms.

Just as she had in her bedroom, she sensed that commanding aura around him. A strength and a depth of passion that she'd been craving for so long, yet had never found in any of her previous lovers.

This was a man strong enough to take her firmly in hand and make all of her fantasies come true.

"Yes," she whispered hungrily. Breathlessly. "Tell me what you're going to do."

* * *

When she woke again, it was to the sound of a childish voice raised in outrage.

"You did the crossword puzzle. I get to do the matching game!"

"No, you don't," one of the other boys piped up. "It's my turn to pick, you have to wait until last, because you got first pick on the Lucky Charms!"

"Stop it! You both have to wait until I finish the crossword puzzle!"

Heidi clutched at her ears, then kicked out with one foot, hoping to connect with Jerome's shin and wake him up to go referee. But she only struck empty air.

Rolling over, she confirmed that she was alone in the bed.

Squinting against the sunlight pouring in through the window, she made sure that he wasn't hidden in some corner, waiting to see how she'd respond to the argument escalating in the kitchen. But he was nowhere in sight.

Had his homecoming last night been a dream after all?

From the next room, it sounded like the boys might soon resort to bloodshed.

She scowled furiously and kicked off the covers. Pulling on her clothes, she yanked on the ankle brace, wincing as the rough gesture earned a painful protest from her injured limb.

Then she hobbled to the bedroom door and slammed it open with enough force to rattle the windows.

"What the...!" She found herself instinctively biting off the curse before it ever reached her lips. No matter how angry she was, swearing at kids just wasn't something she could do.

"What is the problem out here?" She demanded, scowling at each of their startled faces in turn.

The boys hesitated, looking over her shoulder with much more fear than they were looking at her.

Their intensity made her want to look too, but she knew that nobody was there.

"Look at me when I'm talking to you," she commanded. "I don't know what kind of crap your nanny usually puts up with, but I really don't appreciate being dragged out of bed this early to break up a fight. You're brothers. You're genetically obliged to love and care for each other, not beat each other up over a cereal box."

"Hey, our dad says that too," one of the boys grinned, as if she'd just spoken some magic password, which automatically made her a member of some secret club.

"Did you sleep in his bed?" A second boy asked, glancing over her shoulder again.

"Yes," she answered honestly. She saw no reason to lie, especially when they'd just seen her emerge from Jerome's room.

"He's going to be mad," the third boy informed her solemnly. "You're supposed to sleep in the small room, beside ours."

"I'm not your nanny," she pointed out, joining them in the kitchen so she could search for coffee grounds. All of the wine she'd drunk last night was making this conversation more painful than it needed to be. "Do any of you know where the coffee is?"

Instantly, all three boys jumped up to help her. Apparently, they weren't always little monsters, she thought with an amused grin. They not only found the coffee for her, they were eagerly attempting to fill up the pot and set it to percolating.

She would undoubtedly be getting a bitter brew full of spilt grounds, but she thought they were too cute to complain about it.

"Thank you," she smiled, as one of the boys found her a large mug in the cupboard.

"This one is my favorite, because it has a cat on it. See?"

"That is a very handsome cat," she assured him.

Another boy pulled the coffee pot out while it was still attempting to fill and struggled to empty it in her cup without burning himself. About half of the dark liquid ended up on the counter.

"Here, let me help," she urged, but he quickly pulled the pot away.

"I can do it," he assured her, shoving it back onto the base so it could continue filling. "I help Daddy sometimes when he's late for work."

Heidi glanced at the clock, then quickly back to the boys.

"That reminds me, it's almost eight-thirty. Do you have school today?"

"The bus!" Three small voices shouted all at once. Then they were racing for the backpacks which had been dropped beside their chairs as they'd eaten breakfast.

"Come on, hurry!" They called to her.

"What... where...?" Heidi gasped, but the next instant she was being dragged out into the hall. With one bare foot and one in an awkward, thickly soled boot, she was forced into a bouncy trot as they pushed and pulled her to the elevator.

She still had a partially filled coffee mug clenched in one hand, but there was nowhere for her to put it down now. She could only do her best to avoid spilling the hot liquid all over one or more of her diminutive shepherds.

They reached the ground floor, and the moment the elevator doors opened, the boys again began tugging and pushing her along between them.

In a desperate attempt to avoid coffee burns, the next time they paused, she quickly chugged the grainy mixture lining the bottom of her cup.

She must have made one helluva face as she swallowed the ghastly brew, because she looked up to see a small group of parents and children staring at her.

Or maybe it was her appearance that left them gawking. They probably didn't see many barefoot, makeup-smudged, and tangle-haired babysitters down here in the lobby of such a prestigious residence.

She didn't bother asking. The big yellow school bus was pulling up to the curb, and the parents were suddenly too busy kissing and waving to all of their offspring.

Heidi cautiously peeked down at the triplets, but they were already galloping towards the vehicle's open door. As they clamored up the steps and into the bus, she saw them all grinning and waving at her.

She waved back, getting a stupid grin on her face as well. They were sure happy little monsters, even though their dad had pretty much dumped them on a complete stranger last night.

Where was Jerome? Why hadn't he at least called home to check on the boys?

She waited until the school bus was pulling away from the sidewalk and carrying the boys off to school, then she turned and hobbled her way back to the elevator.

A few of the other parents rode up with her, but none

of them appeared too eager to talk with the crazy lady with the clunky black boot and frizzy sleep hair.

There was only one other person remaining in the elevator as Heidi stepped out onto the fourteenth floor. A dark-haired guy that she didn't recognize, but he wasn't really the sort of man she'd have overlooked under normal circumstances.

He was built tall and thick, like a grizzly bear, with a surly expression that put a tremor of fear in her stomach and had her scrubbing damp palms against her thighs.

She tried to shrug off the feeling that he was staring at her.

After her experience with Craig, she knew she could be paranoid. Not all men were evil. She needed to get over this irrational fear of being trapped whenever she was alone in a small, confined area with a male.

Still, she breathed easier when the elevator doors opened, and she was able to escape out into the wide foyer beyond.

It wasn't until she turned the corner, that she felt her stomach clench once more. The front door to Jerome's apartment had been left wide open.

She told herself that in their haste to rush her down to meet the bus, the boys must have failed to close it behind them. But she was already creeped out from the guy on the elevator, and the little hairs on the back of her neck were now standing straight up in alarm.

Her pace slowed to a reluctant limp as she drew closer, afraid of what she might find inside, although she continued to tell herself that the fear was unnecessary.

She hadn't heard of any crime occurring in the building. The owners required deep background checks into every resident when they applied for an apartment. The screening procedure helped weed out potential troublemakers, or those with less than savory friends or relatives.

But it wasn't a fool proof process, her subconscious

nagged at her. And there was no reason for security to prevent a stranger from entering or riding the elevator, unless they somehow raised suspicion.

The building had a few hidden cameras about, but that wouldn't stop a real criminal.

Heidi swallowed and forcefully shoved that thought from her mind.

Why would anyone want to rob a single dad? Jerome's apartment was one of the nicer ones in the building, but with three destructive sons to care for, he hadn't spent much money on expensive electronics or other high-value items which might attract a thief.

Surely, professional burglars would have realized this when they started scouted the building. They would have headed straight up to the penthouse suites on the fifteenth floor.

Despite all reason, she still hesitated in the open doorway.

The boys hadn't bothered to place their bowls in the sink before they'd left, and there was spilled cereal scattered across the table and floor from their arguing.

Two colorful boxes of the breakfast food still sat on the table, but one was now obviously empty and lying on its side. There was also a carton of milk, which the boys had forgotten to return to the fridge.

Otherwise, the apartment looked pretty much the same way it had when she'd arrived the night before. At least, what she could see of it.

Frustrated, she scowled at the walls which blocked her view of the interior rooms.

She couldn't exactly leave the door open while she went to investigate potential hiding places. That sort of behavior might allow someone to sneak in behind her. But she really hated the idea of closing herself into a place where she couldn't be sure whether she was alone. This was exactly the sort of scenario which had driven her into an open floor loft.

For at least the millionth time since it had happened, she cursed Craig for what he had turned her into. She'd never had these fears before she'd walked into Morgan's house that day and found herself the victim of a deranged and violent drug addict.

With a sigh of frustration, she reached for the phone that was usually snug in her pocket, but realized she'd left it lying on the table beside Jerome's bed.

"Damn it..." The curse was broken off by an enormous hand, which closed over the lower half of her face, shutting off all air through her mouth and nose. A second hand snaked around her waist, even as a living wall of hard muscle propelled her forward into the apartment.

She was so shocked and terrified, it took her brain several long seconds to realize that her worst nightmare was actually coming true. By then, he had her inside the apartment and was kicking the door shut behind them.

A black haze swam at the edges of her vision as her lungs began to scream from the lack of oxygen. The stark terror and adrenaline now pumping through her system was all that kept her from collapsing in her attacker's arms.

Then she was being thrown violently towards the center of the room, stumbling over the awkward ankle brace - and her own feet - in a desperate attempt to right herself.

Spinning around, she came eye to eye with the black barrel of a monstrous handgun. And glowering down at her from behind the weapon, was the surly grizzly bear from the elevator.

"He's not here," an unfamiliar male voice spoke up from the direction of the hallway, but Heidi found it impossible to tear her eyes away from the gun.

She'd seen a few firearms in her life, but never one so close. And never one pointed at her head. It summoned up a depth of terror unlike anything she'd ever experienced, not even when she'd been Craig's prisoner.

During those terrible hours, she'd been terrified, but

only because of the pain he was inflicting. This new fear was awakened by the very real possibility of dying.

"Where is he?" The grizzly holding the gun growled in a deep voice that sounded as if he gargled razor blades for breakfast.

But Heidi couldn't answer. All rational thought had fled the moment she'd found herself staring into the black hole of his weapon.

The huge man stepped closer, taking a fist full of her t-shirt, and using it to hold her in place as he pressed the cold metal barrel of the gun directly to her forehead.

"Where is the Fed bastard who lives here?"

CHAPTER SIX

Fed?

Heidi struggled to understand what they were asking of her.

"I don't know," she pleaded, and it was true. She had no clue what they were talking about. All of this had to be some kind of huge, terrible mistake.

Worse, she was in very real danger of fainting, which might be just the nudge her captor needed to put a bullet between her eyes.

"We're not idiots," that unseen man behind her pointed out. "You're the nanny. He wouldn't leave his kids with you and not give you some way to call him, in case of an emergency."

Heidi would have shaken her head, but she was too afraid of jostling the deadly weapon being held against her.

"I'm not his nanny," she managed in a strained whisper. "She never showed up, so I got stuck with the boys. I'm just a neighbor, that's all. He never gave me any information. I don't even know his last name."

The grizzly with the gun didn't look convinced. In fact, he looked even meaner and angrier than before.

"You're lying," he growled.

"No, I swear, it's true," she gasped, feeling cold metal grinding against her skull. "I don't have any reason to lie to you."

"It doesn't matter anyway," the man behind her suggested. "We'll just wait here until he shows up."

Heidi felt ice crystals forming in her blood. In just a few short hours, school would be over, and the boys would be coming home. If these men were still here, the boys might be hurt. Or worse.

She couldn't let that happen. Although she'd only known them a short time, she knew they were good kids. Hell, who was she kidding? Even if they had been juvenile delinquents, she would never wish anything like this upon them.

Having already lived through this kind of nightmare once before, she knew how it could destroy someone's life. She couldn't allow the boys to suffer the way that she had. The way she was still suffering, if she was being honest with herself.

Which meant she needed to get rid of these creeps before the boys showed up. Or she needed to escape and intercept the children before they reached the apartment.

Despite the helplessness of her situation, she felt a surge of adrenaline and anger. It swallowed up all but the ragged edges of her fear, and somehow made everything around her appear clearer.

Grizzly gave a low grunt, then withdrew the monstrous gun and tucked it into his waistband, just like in every bad gangster movie she'd ever seen.

Her gaze cut quickly to the door behind him, but with the gawky boot on her leg, she knew she'd never make it past the man. Her only hope was to bide her time and wait for an opportunity to escape.

"Have a seat," he rumbled, as if it were perfectly reasonable for him to threaten her life one minute and be a gentleman in the next.

She hesitated, hoping that he'd go find a place to sit

himself, leaving her a clear path to the exit. But the guy wasn't as stupid as she'd hoped.

"That wasn't an invitation," he stated much more aggressively, and she decided it would be wise to obey.

Rather than walking into the living area to sit on the couch, she turned towards the hard kitchen chairs. They were closer to the door, and would provide her with a solid launching pad, if the opportunity for escape should present itself.

The move also allowed her to get a look at the second man, who was still standing in the doorway to Jerome's bedroom.

If the first man was a grizzly bear, then this one was a weasel. His face was narrow and sharply angled. He was also shorter and very thin, with inky black hair and dark dangerous looking eyes, which were currently focused upon a small stack of loose papers clasped in his hands.

A glimpse into the room beyond, left her slack jawed. The floor was covered several inches deep with piles of clothing, paperwork, and unrecognizable litter.

"Did you find something?" Grizzly asked, but the weasel ignored him, making Heidi suspect that the smaller man was actually the leader of the two.

What possible reason could men such as these want with Jerome? They'd called him a Fed, but she was pretty sure you couldn't be a single dad and an FBI agent.

Maybe this was just a huge case of mistaken identity. But that didn't make the situation any less terrifying. She'd seen both of their faces. In the movies, that meant they would have to kill her, to keep her from ratting them out.

Oh, dear goddess, why had she watched so many crime dramas? It gave her imagination too many terrible ideas now.

"Look, guys, I'm not even supposed to be here," she attempted to reason with them. "That asshole told me the nanny would be showing up last night. I don't want anything to do with him, or you, or whatever the hell is going on here. So, if you don't mind, I'd really like to go back home now and totally forget that any of this ever happened."

After I've ambushed the boys at the bus stop and taken them to a safe place, she silently added.

"Sorry, Sweetcheeks. We might need you to manage the little brats for us, while we wait for their daddy," Weasel chuckled, without looking up from his papers.

She got the impression he'd found her suggestion mildly amusing, but otherwise considered her value to be somewhere between a mop and a toilet brush. She was nothing more than a tool that he intended to use and discard.

Abruptly, the thin man cursed and threw the papers to the floor.

Muttering something under his breath, he turned and headed down the hall. Apparently, he intended to search the other rooms in the apartment, which left Grizzly as her only guardian.

The larger man had moved to stand on the other side of the kitchen table, pouring himself a bowl of cereal from one of the boxes the boys had left out. He was facing her, but he'd have to run all the way around the table to catch her.

Unless he decided to simply shoot her in the back and avoid the cardio. That thought made the skin prickle all the way down her spine, but she didn't know what else she could do.

There wasn't a silencer on his gun, but the walls were insulated so well, she doubted anyone would report one loud bang.

If they did hear a bang, they'd probably just think the boys had broken something. Unless she was able to reach the door and open it. If he shot her in the hall, that was sure to draw attention.

It might be enough to save the boys, and maybe even herself. If there was one thing all of those crime dramas had taught her, it was that gunshot victims could survive, if they received help in time.

One little bitty gunshot wound couldn't be as bad as what Craig had done to her... right? If she could survive those hellish days trapped with Morgan's home with a lunatic, she could survive anything.

Mentally, she struggled to psyche herself up, but it was hard to think of anything but the pain she knew was coming. Then Grizzly was picking up his cereal bowl, cupping it in one massive hand as he turned to search the nearby drawers for a clean spoon.

Fear and adrenaline spiked through her system as she realized that this was the moment she'd been waiting for.

Shoving herself up off the chair, she bolted for the front door as quickly as her hobbled leg allowed.

For a few breathless heartbeats she actually felt hope swell in her chest. Then something hard struck her right between the shoulder blades and knocked her sprawling onto the floor.

With the awkward weight and size of the brace on her ankle, she struggled to get up off her knees.

Freedom was right there, just a few inches away. She could almost reach the handle.

Then she was struck again, this time in the back of her head, and the whole world went dark.

🐈 CHAPTER SEVEN

Heidi grumbled and attempted to roll away from the tiny hands which were petting her face. She wasn't ready to wake up yet.

"Is she dead?" A small voice asked.

"No, she's still breathing. See?" Another voice answered.

For a moment, Heidi wondered how children could have snuck into her apartment.

Had she left the door unlocked? Not likely, she always triple-checked the bolts on the door and windows before going to sleep. Then the memories came flooding back, and her eyes flashed open with a start.

She wasn't in her bed at home. She was lying on the floor in Jerome's apartment, with three identical little figures crouched beside her, all wearing matching expressions of fear and confusion.

The boys were home from school, but there might still be criminals in the house. Her battered brain attempted to put all of the pieces together. She had to get the boys out before Grizzly and Weasel found them.

Unless it was already too late.

Her gaze rose to search the room behind the children,

and she saw the larger of the two men now seated in the chair she had vacated at the table.

At some point after he'd knocked her into Dreamland, the brute must have dragged her body into the living room area. She was now sprawled on the floor, just to one side of the couch.

There was no sign of the weasel-faced ringleader of the pair. He might still be searching the back rooms, or he could have left altogether.

"Are you alright?" One of the boys murmured, worriedly. "You were having a nightmare. You kept calling for someone named Morgan. Is that your boyfriend?"

"No," Heidi winced as she pushed herself up carefully into a seated position. "Morgan is a girl I know."

Hearing her voice, Grizzly looked up. But he didn't offer more than a bored glance before turning back to the small computer tablet in his hands. Heidi felt her jaw drop open, but quickly closed it again. It was bizarre trying to imagine the burly monster doing something as mundane as checking his email.

"I'm scared," the boy sitting to her right admitted, tears glistening in his eyes. "Are those guys going to hurt our daddy?"

Heidi didn't know what to say. What if Jerome came home before they could escape? Would his sons be forced to watch him suffer, and possibly die? The thought was too terrible to consider.

"It's okay to be scared sometimes," she said softly, to keep her words from being overheard by the thug seated in the kitchen. "But I'm going to do everything I can to protect you and your dad, okay?"

"How?" He whimpered.

Good question, she silently admitted. She couldn't exactly just point her finger and turn their captors into toads. As far as she knew, magic like that didn't really exist. But she might be able to work a different sort of magic here.

She could give the boys a little dose of hope and courage.

"I'll tell you a secret, okay?" She whispered with a confidence she didn't really feel. "I'm actually a witch."

"A good witch," she hurriedly added when the boys gave a combined gasp and leaned back as if suddenly afraid to touch her. "I only cast spells to help or protect people."

"Like Daddy?"

Heidi offered a smile that felt a bit tense but seemed to soothe the boys. "Yes, and the three of you. Now tell me your names again, I need to figure out a way to differentiate between you."

"I'm Jaden, he's Jaxon, and he's Jacob."

Cute. Why did some parents think it was such a great idea to saddle their twins or triplets with such similar monikers? She silently thanked her own mother and father for being sensible.

"Would you boys like to do a tiny little spell with me, right now?" She asked, seeking a way to distract the trio and maybe give them a bit of hope in the process.

She knew from her own time in captivity, how intense and prolonged fear could become the worst kind of hell. She had to do whatever she could to help the boys cope, as well as protect them.

All three looked absolutely fascinated by the idea of doing something magical, which gave her hope.

"I don't have my spell book, or the ingredients for anything big, but we could do a visualization ritual," she suggested with a secretive smile as the boys leaned closer, nodding their heads.

All three were looking up at her with wide-eyed curiosity and hope.

"Will it make the bad guys leave?" One of them asked. It was the boy who'd declared himself as Jaden. He seemed to be the most outgoing in the group, usually taking on the role of spokesperson for their little trio. That personality trait might help her identify him in the future, at least when his brothers were around for comparison.

Heidi gave a small shrug, not wanting to discourage them, but not wanting to lie either.

"It's not going to turn them into toads," she whispered. "But it will help all of us stay brave and strong until the police come to rescue us."

"Okay," Jaden nodded firmly.

"All of you scoot closer and form a small ring," she directed, helping them into place.

Where they were positioned really didn't matter, unless she planned to cast a circle. But she thought the close physical contact might be a helpful reminder of how the boys still had each other, no matter what happened in the next few hours.

"Now hold hands," she instructed. "Do you know what energy is?"

"Daddy says we have energy when we eat too much sugar and run around a lot," Jadon offered solemnly.

Heidi smiled.

"When you cast a magic spell you are filled with energy just like that, but it comes from the earth, and the elements, and other things like that."

The boys looked a little confused.

"Close your eyes," she instructed. "I'll show you what I mean."

The boys quickly obeyed.

"Now, think of a day when you were outside, playing in the sunshine," she guided in a low and gentle tone. "Maybe you're at the beach, or at the park. It's a warm day, but not too hot. It's just right. You can feel the warm rays of sun on your face and arms. They're very soft and soothing, like your favorite pajamas fresh from the dryer."

Around her, the boys' faces were tilted up, as if they could really feel what she was describing. Already they looked more relaxed, their imaginations taking them away from the confines of the apartment to a happier time and place.

"Feel the warmth moving slowly downward as if it were warm honey being poured over your head. Soft warm honey flowing slowly down over your cheeks and onto your shoulders. Then down your arms. Down to each of your fingertips."

She continued to walk them deeper and deeper into the visualization. Her goal wasn't to put them fully into a hypnotic state, but only to help them relax and give them some courage to face what was coming.

Without some kind of miracle, they could be prisoners here for any number of days. Until Jerome came home. But when that happened, the boys would be forced to see their father at the mercy of whatever Grizzly and Weasel had planned for him.

From the way the two men talked, they were angry enough to cause serious pain and possibly even death. There was no way that she could really prepare the boys for that outcome, but she could help ease their fear and help them find strength in each other.

"Whatever you're muttering about, stop it!" Grizzly abruptly barked from the kitchen, startling Heidi so violently she actually reared back as if she'd been struck.

The burly man's growl had an even more profound effect on the boys. They'd been deep in a happy, almost trance-like state when he'd snapped at them. His angry voice both shattered their fantasy and yanked them brutally back to the present, in one sharp moment.

All three boys launched up onto their feet, eyes wide and white-rimmed with terror. They looked on the verge of running away, but there was nowhere for them to run. They were trapped, cornered like mice by a monstrous man with a gun.

"It's okay boys," Heidi murmured gently, realizing that her intentions had backfired horribly.

If Grizzly had just kept his mouth shut for just a few more minutes, she could have finished what she'd been doing with the boys, and the youngsters wouldn't have been caught in a vulnerable sub-trance state.

But the brute with the gun had spoken up at exactly the wrong moment, when the boys were most susceptible to emotions and suggestions. Now they were even more frightened than before, and she wasn't sure if she could calm them down enough to try again. Or if they'd feel comfortable enough to try.

"I won't let anyone hurt you," Heidi soothed them in the same low tone she'd used to guide them earlier.

"I said shut up!" Grizzly roared, lurching to his feet as if he meant to come over and silence her permanently. One of his hands even dropped to the butt of the pistol still snugged in the waistband of his pants.

Heidi threw up her hands, as if she meant to physically catch any bullets before they could reach the boys. But she was no longer surrounded by children.

At first, she thought they had bolted, but there was nowhere for them to hide.

Looking down in confusion, she was startled to see three yellow kittens drowning in discarded clothing.

The tiny felines hissed and spat. Their backs were sharply arched in fear, and all the fur on their tails and bodies was sticking straight up in every direction. It gave them the appearance of being little yellow puff balls. They would have been adorable, if one didn't consider their shocking mutation from human form.

Grizzly was just as dumbfounded as she was, if not more so. He made the sign of the cross over his enormous chest half a dozen times, chanting a Latin prayer that Heidi didn't understand.

His face was white as a sheet, and he now appeared every bit as horrified as the boys had looked only moments before.

Before the man could regain his composure, Heidi grabbed the hem of her shirt and pulled it up to make a little kangaroo pouch. She then snatched up all three snarling little felines and plopped them inside, before scrambling for the nearest doorway.

Jerome's room had been totally destroyed during Weasel's search, but she managed to shove the door shut and lock it behind her. Leaning up against the wooden barrier, she frantically tried to think of what she should do next.

What the hell had she done to the boys? She hadn't even cast a circle, much less a spell. But how else could the boys have been transformed? This had to be some kind of magic, but she'd never believed this level of sorcery was actually possible.

Maybe it was a magical version of a mother lifting a car off from her fallen child? Some subconscious power that she'd summoned up in a desire to protect three helpless little boys. It sounded insane, even to her, but how could she argue with the proof squirming furiously inside of her makeshift pouch?

Worse, how was she supposed to protect them now? They were so tiny, even a small fall might kill one.

She looked at the bedroom window as that thought struck her.

They were on the fourteenth floor. A fall from this height was suicide, but cats were supposed to be agile right? Hurrying over, she found that the window had the same type of bolting locks as the panes in her apartment.

Quickly she released the lock bolts and shoved the glass open. It was designed to only open so far, preventing a child from climbing out onto the ledge. She would certainly never fit, but the little fur balls clutched inside her shirt could.

"May the God and Goddess protect you," she whispered fearfully, as a loud, thunderous crack warned that grizzly had recovered from his shock and was about to break down the bedroom door.

Clawing desperately at the screen covering the open window, she failed to pry it out, but did succeed in tearing the mesh out of its metal frame in one corner. It might be just big enough. Pulling one of the kittens out of her shirt, she threaded the tiny figure through the hole and placed him on the ledge that ran beneath the outside of the window.

"If you can understand me, then run and hide," she gasped, pulling a second and third kitten from her shirt and shoving them out through the hole to join their brother. "I'll find you again, and I promise I'll try to make things right."

The words were hardly out of her mouth before the door crashed open and Grizzly was aiming his monstrous gun at her.

"Change them back!" He roared.

Heidi stole a quick look over her shoulder, but the ledge was empty. The boys were gone. She prayed she could uphold her end of the promise, but at least they were safe, for now.

"They're gone," she cried, with some of her former spirit restored. "You'll never see them again, and if you don't let me go, I'll do the same thing to you."

"Like hell you will!"

The roar of the gun was deafening.

CHAPTER EIGHT

Heidi instinctively cowered, but the bullet missed her and embedded itself into the sheetrock nearby.

"What the hell are you doing?" Weasel's voice was hardly audible through the ringing in Heidi's ears. Looking up from where she'd fallen beneath the window, she saw the two men fighting for control of the gun.

Grizzly was wild eyed and staring at her as if she were the devil itself. But as powerful as the larger man was, Weasel had speed and technique. The smaller man twisted the gun against his opponent's thumb and tore it from the Grizzly's grasp.

"Are you insane?" Weasel was furious. "The window is open, you idiot! What if someone heard the shot? We have to get out of here before the police arrive. Where are the kids?"

"She turned them into cats!" Grizzly howled.

"What?" Weasel looked ready to slap his companion. Instead, he turned to Heidi. "Where are they?"

She clenched her jaw and scowled at him, but Grizzly quickly answered. "She threw them out the window. They're gone. We have nothing left to bargain with. She's cost us everything!"

The weasel's eyes flashed from where Heidi was now seated on the floor, to the open window, with its torn screen, above her. Then to the bullet hole, which was still smoking sheetrock dust.

"There's no time to explain," he snarled furiously. "Grab the girl. We might have to leverage our way out."

"Hell no!" Grizzly immediately retreated a step and crossed his chest again. "She's a witch. You didn't see what she did to those kids."

"God damn it, you superstitious idiot, you do what I say, or I'll kill you both!"

Heidi did her best to look intimidating, but Weasel apparently scared the big man more. One massive paw lashed out to seize a handful of her hair, and he used it to pull her to her feet.

"You say anything, even one word, and I'll snap your neck," he growled. "Got it, witch?"

From the look on his face, it might not even take that much. The man's hands were trembling as he steered her towards the front door.

Weasel made a gesture, and Grizzly traded his grip in her hair for a thick arm wrapped around her shoulders, almost like a lover.

"One word," he repeated, now directly against her left temple.

Weasel opened the front door, and they were moving. The smaller man walked behind Heidi. Although she couldn't see it, she was sure that the barrel of the gun he'd taken from Grizzly was now pointed at her back.

They reached the elevator without seeing anyone, and she suddenly realized how dire her situation was.

If these men successfully escaped with her, they would almost certainly kill her soon after. Her only chance at survival was to escape now, while she might still gain some help from the police or other residents in the building.

But how could she possibly break free of Grizzly's grasp, without getting shot in the back?

Although she'd previously considered getting shot as a viable option, now that the boys were relatively out of danger, she found her courage lacking.

The elevator doors opened, and Grizzly shoved her inside. Weasel followed and took up a position near the buttons. He still held the gun pointed in her general direction, but at least she could see it now.

What if she tried kicking the weapon out of his hands, the way they did in the movies? With this boot on her ankle, she'd probably end up on her ass, and still get shot.

The elevator doors started to close, and her panic rose.

It was as if she were watching all hope vanish along with the artificial light from the foyer beyond.

Just before the doors sealed shut, an enormous yellow cat darted inside and skidded to a nervous halt in the middle of the elevator floor. Heidi and her captors all stared down at it in surprise, while the feline looked up at each of them in wary suspicion.

The dark golden hair along the ridge of the creature's spine was slightly raised, as was the fur down the length of its tail. From the confused expression on its face, the feline hadn't intended to jump aboard, and was now feeling trapped and frightened.

If she'd been alone in the elevator, Heidi might have crouched and attempted to soothe the creature. She seen plenty of cats get into trouble following their curiosity, or a game of chasing invisible dust motes.

That made her think of the three little kittens she'd so recently sent scurrying out the window and left her worrying about what might happen to them now.

She might have saved them from Grizzly and Weasel, but she'd also left them alone and vulnerable. They were as helpless and defenseless as this cat, but much smaller and weaker. What if she didn't survive her captivity this time? Where would they go? How would they survive?

What if they ended up in the pound?

No, she couldn't allow herself to consider that horrible

possibility. She had to focus on escaping and finding them again.

Although she wasn't sure how they'd transformed into cats, she was certain that Morgan and Rachel could help her find a way to turn them back into boys.

Morgan had her grandmother's old spell book, packed full of rituals and magical notations. There had to be something in there about shapeshifting. But if there wasn't, Heidi would keep looking until she found a cure.

The enormous cat at her feet made a low rumbling sound, something halfway between a meow and a growl.

Weasel had turned back to watch the numbers counting down on the little panel beside the door, but Grizzly was still scowling down at the animal. There was a dangerous look in his eyes, suggesting that he too was recalling the boys' supernatural means of escape, and he now considered all felines suspect.

The cat must have sensed a threat in the burly man's stare, because it moved to crouch against the wall farthest from the thug, glowering up from within Heidi's shadow. Then they were arriving on the ground floor and every eye in the elevator was drawn to the opening doors.

If Heidi was going to escape, this might be her only chance. But that realization appeared to strike Grizzly and Weasel at the same time.

Grizzly whirled around, catching Heidi off guard as he surged forward, crushing her body up against the back wall of the elevator. His mouth came down over hers... hard. This was not a kiss, this was a violent smothering of her voice, to keep her from crying out to whomever was on the other side of that door.

Unseen by any viewer, one of his burly hands was clenched around her throat, promising instant retribution if she tried anything stupid. Weasel had stepped forward to block the entrance to the elevator.

"Hey there slugger," the gunman smiled down at someone Heidi couldn't see from over Grizzly's shoulder.

"Where are your parents? Sorry, but we don't have room for anyone else at the moment. You'll have to wait for the next elevator, alright?"

Then the doors were closing again, but as they drew together, Heidi saw something that gave her small rush of hope.

A police car was pulling up to the curb outside the large double glass doors that led to the apartment lobby. But why weren't they flashing their lights or sounding the siren? And shouldn't there be more than one car? Didn't a gunshot inspire a bigger response than this one solitary patrol vehicle?

Then it struck her, and her heart sank. The police had received a 911 call, but they didn't believe that it was actually a gunshot.

The officers would go upstairs to talk to whomever had placed the call. They'd file a report and perhaps talk to a few of the neighbors, to discover if any of them had seen or heard anything. But by the time anyone figured out what had really happened, Heidi and her kidnappers would be long gone.

Almost as soon as the elevator doors were closed, Grizzly shoved away from her and turned to Weasel.

"Gimme back my gun," he snarled. "I don't trust that witch."

"Not a chance. You'll just fire off another round and alert the cops to exactly where we are," Weasel answered in the same patronizing tone he'd used on the child who'd summoned the elevator to the ground floor.

Grizzly made a sound much like the animal he resembled. It was a deep, throaty growl that resonated up from his chest in a way that seemed to fill the tiny area around Heidi with dread.

"You gimme back my gun, or I'm walking away. You can bloody finish this job by yourself."

"If you try to walk, I'll put a bullet in your back, or the boss will send someone to do us both. Just shut up and watch the girl, you superstitious ass. You've already cost us our only leverage over the fed. He's not going to fall into line without those boys," Weasel snarled back. "We'll have to lean on another member of the team. There will be too many eyes on this guy now."

Heidi didn't understand what they were talking about, but it sounded as if they were giving up on Jerome. She was glad for that, but she feared their decision may have come too late for her or the boys.

How long could three little kittens survive alone on the streets? If she were killed, or unable to find them again…

Heidi had to force the thought from her mind. It was too terrible to consider. Although she'd only recently met the triplets, it felt as though they'd survived an entire lifetime together. She cared for them now, more than she'd ever believed herself capable.

There had to be a way for her to escape and find them. But how? She had no weapons, and she was hobbled by a leg brace. In despair, she glanced down at the awkward boot on her ankle, but a motion in the corner of the elevator drew her gaze.

To her surprise, the big yellow cat hadn't escaped onto the first floor. He was still crouched in one far corner, glowering up at the two men arguing near the doors. The poor creature must be waiting for the thugs to exit before making his own escape.

Someone had once told her that animals could sense evil intent in humans. As she watched the cat, she could believe that it was true.

Abruptly, the elevator stopped, and the doors were opening once more. They'd reached the garage.

Grizzly and Weasel tensed as they waited to see if the subterranean level was swarming with police officers blocking their escape, but there was not a single badge in sight. Heidi's last hope was now gone.

"Grab the girl," Weasel commanded as he stepped forward to hold the doors open and watch for any sign of a patrol car entering the area.

She steeled herself for a fight. This was her last stand. If she was going to die, she might as well do it on her own terms. Yet just as Grizzly was turning to grab her, a huge figure reared up from the shadows.

She never saw the newcomer's face and had no time to consider how he might have arrived inside a sealed elevator car. She could only stare in shock as one powerful fist shot out to strike Grizzly in the jaw, sending the larger man stumbling backwards into Weasel.

Both men fell beneath the impact and the gun went flying.

There were three men grappling for the fallen weapon as the elevator doors began to close, with Heidi still inside.

🐈 CHAPTER NINE

For several long moments, Heidi could only stare in amazement at the emptiness surrounding her.

She was free!

But how? Looking up at the ceiling of the elevator car, she expected to see a roof panel removed or some other opening through which a large man might have dropped in. Only, there were no holes, no gaps, and no possible explanation for his sudden appearance.

She was still staring at the ceiling in open-mouthed confusion, when the elevator began moving again. Someone upstairs must have called it. Perhaps even the boy that Weasel had chased away.

It didn't matter. She remembered seeing the patrol car pulling up to the curb in front of the complex, and it spurred her into action. Stumbling forward, she quickly started stabbing at the ground floor button on the panel. Punching the little dot over and over in rapid succession, as if she could speed up the machinery through sheer desperation.

Time seemed to stand still, the elevator dragging along at its terribly reliable pace. Then the doors were finally opening, and she was looking up into the bored faces of two uniformed police officers.

It didn't matter that one was short, chubby and balding. Or that the other was wearing at least one size too large, giving the appearance of a gawky teenager trying on his father's clothes. To her, they looked like angels, sent straight from heaven.

"Hurry, hurry, they're in the garage!" She was already stabbing at the button on the panel once more, giving the officers no choice but to ride down to the subterranean level with her.

"They were going to kill me and the boys, but he's fighting them. They have guns. He's going to be killed. You have to stop them!" Heidi didn't realize how hysterical she sounded, as she began repeating the information over and over, but after just a moment of consideration, both men appeared to believe her.

Maybe that was because she was now sobbing like a baby.

She was saved. She would live. And the boys were going to be safe. As soon as Grizzly and Weasel were in handcuffs, she'd go find the little fur-babies and do whatever it took to change them back into children.

As relieved as she was, the tears would not stop. Yet, all too soon, the elevator had reached the underground parking level and the doors were beginning to open.

The taller of the two officers, ordered her to stay back as both men unsnapped their holsters and prepared themselves for whatever might be waiting on the other side.

Ignoring the command, Heidi held her ground in the center of the lift. She needed to see what happened, to know that the Grizzly and Weasel were captured and no longer a threat to the triplets.

If the thugs were already gone, she would never find the closure she needed.

An apartment without interior doors and walls would never be enough to soothe her fears then. She'd have to leave Aspire, her family, and her friends. She'd have to change her identity and spend the rest of her life watching over her shoulder for a bullet that may or may not ever be coming for her.

One of the officers uttered a startled oath and Heidi found herself staring in open mouthed disbelief.

Weasel and Grizzly were both lying on the ground just outside the elevator doors. The fallen gun was nearby, as was a large and frightening looking knife. But both men were unconscious.

There was no sign of the man that had done this to them.

"Those are the men that held me and the boys hostage," Heidi quickly proclaimed, fighting an urge to shove the officers forward, hurrying them to handcuff the fallen men before they awakened. "There was another man here. He saved me, but I didn't see his face. He was fighting them when the elevator doors closed and took me upstairs to meet you."

"You're sure that these are the men?" The bald officer asked.

"Of course I'm sure! The bigger one shot at me with that gun. There is a hole upstairs in the wall where he missed, but they would have killed me as soon as they were sure they'd escaped. The smaller one said they only needed me for leverage," her voice was cold and hard, despite the tears still wet on her cheeks.

That appeared to be enough for the officers. One of them snapped handcuffs onto the unconscious men, while the other radioed for back up.

"We'll have to read them their rights when they wake up. It looks like they sure took a beating," the scrawny officer mused. "Can you describe the guy that did this to them?"

She shook her head.

"I'm not even sure where he came from," she admitted. "That big guy was about to drag me out of the elevator, then… oh! I just remembered something. He was naked. The guy that attacked them was completely naked."

It was strange, she hadn't even registered her rescuer's nudity until that moment. Her fear and the shock of seeing him appear out of thin air had made the moment so surreal, she hadn't considered his lack of clothing.

The two uniformed men glanced at each other.

"Would you like for us to call an ambulance?" One asked. "You've had a bad shock. You might want to get checked out."

She could understand their skepticism, but she didn't care what they might think. All that mattered, was that Grizzly and Weasel were in handcuffs. She, Jerome, and the boys were all safe.

"Oh my goddess! I forgot about the boys," she gasped, spinning around to punch the button for the elevator. "I need to get back upstairs. I was babysitting three little boys. I...I helped them hide, so these guys wouldn't hurt them. But I need to get back up there and make sure that they're okay."

"One of us should probably go with you," the taller officer suggested. "But I don't want to leave Officer Brown alone to watch both men. If you wait just a moment, we'll have additional officers available. Then I'll escort you upstairs."

Heidi felt a whisper of fear raise the tiny hairs on the back of her neck. Even with the gun and the knife to testify to the violent nature of the two men in custody, she thought her accusations against them might lose strength if she explained the real reason she was looking for three yellow kittens, instead of actual children.

She'd been practicing magic for a while now, yet even she had not believed in the possibility of physical transformation. She still wasn't sure exactly what had happened during those terrifying moments just after Grizzly had interrupted their meditation, but she was certain these cops would never believe her.

"No, I can't wait. I'm sorry, but the boys are too young to be left alone. Its apartment, 14C. We won't touch anything in the apartment. I'll just go find them and take them down to my apartment, which is 13B. We'll wait for you there."

He started to shake his head, but she wasn't about to surrender on this point. As soon as the elevator doors opened, she was hurrying inside.

"Please, Officer... Varian," she begged, with a quick glance at his name tag. "They must be scared out of their wits right now."

He hesitated a moment too long and the elevator was leaving without him. He wasn't going to be very happy about her escape, but Heidi really needed to get upstairs and find the boys, without any police complication.

A few moments later, as she hobbled off onto the fourteenth floor, she could see that the front door to the apartment was still wide open. An older woman was standing in the hallway just outside, wringing her hands in distress.

Heidi hurried forward.

"Has Jerome returned?"

The old woman started, her eyes widening.

"Have you seen him or the boys? I heard a gunshot. And look at this mess! I called the police, but they haven't arrived yet. What could be taking them so long? Oh, those poor boys."

Heidi shook her head and pushed past, into the apartment.

"Jerome left the boys with me," she explained, as the older woman followed her nervously inside. "There were two men here. One of them shot at me, there."

She gestured at the bedroom wall, as she hobbled straight to the window and looked out at the ledge beyond. It was empty. There was not a single kitten in sight.

Her stomach sank.

"Oh no! Oh no, that is awful," the old woman gasped.

"Where are the boys now? Where is Jerome? What about those men? How did you get away?"

"The police have our kidnappers downstairs, in handcuffs," Heidi assured her, tearing out more of the window screen so that she could stick her head out of the tiny opening and take a better look in both directions.

The ledge was empty, but it wrapped around the entire building. The boys must have followed it out of sight, probably frightened by the sound of the gun firing.

She pushed away from the window and clunked back out into the hallway, with the old woman still following and asking questions that Heidi was no longer willing to answer. She needed to focus on finding the boys before the police came looking for them.

When she'd placed the boys on the ledge, they'd been on the eastern side of the window. If they'd continued in that direction, she might be able to see them from the window in the guest room at the far end of the apartment.

It wasn't until she was hurrying past the boys' bedroom, that she realized that she and the old woman weren't alone in the apartment. A tiny noise drew her attention to the boys' door, which was now cracked just a hair.

As she stopped to look, the door opened just a bit more, and she saw a tiny little face peeking out from behind it.

A very human face.

"Jaden?" She gasped, guessing correctly.

Instantly, the boy threw the door open and rushed out to embrace her.

His brothers were quick to follow, nearly knocking her flat on her ass. But she was just as happy to see them, and quickly dropped down to her knees so she could pull them all into her arms.

She heard the woman behind her sending prayers of gratitude to the angels, the saints, her god, and anyone else that might be listening. And Heidi had half a mind to join her. Whatever magical curse or blessing the children might have been under when she'd left, it appeared to have worn off.

And just in time.

"Are these the boys?" A male voice asked from nearby.

A glance over Heidi's shoulder revealed that Officer Varian had waited only long enough for the elevator to return to the parking level, before following her up.

"Yes," she assured him, but she didn't let go of the triplets.

"Just tell them you hid under your dad's bed," she spoke in an almost silent whisper as she gave the boys another hug. Then she stood to face Officer Varian and the worried neighbor, praying that the kids understood. And that their answers would hold up under interrogation, if it came to that.

If Grizzly claimed he'd seen her turn the boys into kittens, the officers would think he was crazy. But if the boys made the same claim, the legal process was going to get a whole lot more complicated. Nobody would believe them, of course. But there would be a lot more questions about what had really happened.

"Are you boys alright?" Officer Varian questioned, in a slightly gentler tone.

The boys just nodded and pressed closer to Heidi's legs. They looked unwilling to answer any questions, no matter how innocent.

"What about you?" Officer Varian nodded towards the elderly neighbor. "Were you here when it happened?"

"No," she quickly shook her head. "But I live next door. I'm the one that heard the gunshot and called you."

"Alright then, I'll need to get statements from each of you," the uniformed man suggested. "I'll also need you all to step out of the apartment, until after the forensic team is able to take some pictures and recover the bullet."

"Jaden! Jaxon! Jacob!" Jerome's voice brought Heidi's gaze up with a start and summoned a resonate shout of joy from all three boys.

In an instant, the triplets had shoved past Officer Varian and the older woman beside him, to launch themselves into their father's open arms. The sight brought Heidi's heart up into her throat, even as relief flooded through her body.

Jerome was safe and he was home. She'd never been so glad to see a man in all of her life. But she also felt a twinge of regret. She was in lust with the father, but she now cared for the boys. What if Jerome pushed her away once more?

She caught his gaze for only a moment, before Officer Varian was demanding his attention, asking him an endless number of questions. But in that one moment, she saw nothing that might give her hope.

Jerome looked exhausted, distressed, and upset by what he'd come home to discover.

Dark shadows under his eyes suggested that he hadn't slept well during his absence from the apartment.

Was it possible that Grizzly and Weasel were right? Was he really a federal officer? Or had he simply been missing his sons? The latter seemed much more likely, but after all that had happened, she just couldn't be sure.

Additional officers quickly arrived to take pictures of the mess and retrieve the bullet that Grizzly had fired at Heidi.

They also took a few quick photos of the massive goose egg on the back of Heidi's head.

But not once did they give her a chance to speak to the Jerome alone. She could only watch him holding his sons, comforting them, and silently wish that she too belonged within his embrace.

CHAPTER TEN

"Alright, it looks like we're through here," Varian approached Heidi sometime later. "Would you like me to walk you down to your apartment and assure that everything there is in order?"

She considered returning to her apartment alone, and mentally cringed. She was going to struggle making that initial journey by herself, but she wasn't yet ready to leave Jerome or the boys.

It was sometime after nine o'clock. The elderly woman from next door had left hours ago.

The triplets had given up on anyone making them a real dinner. They were now seated at the kitchen table, helping themselves to some of the cereal, which had been left out since breakfast.

Jerome was standing with his back to Heidi, staring at the destruction in his bedroom. She wanted to run to his side and comfort him, but she didn't feel as though he might welcome such a gesture.

Still, she needed to at least be near him. Just for a little while longer. Just until she was able to convince herself that this whole nightmare was really over. And maybe get a chance to explain to Jerome how she now felt.

"Thank you," She finally answered the uniformed man beside her a weary smile. "But I think I'll stay."

Varian looked a bit disappointed, but he quickly excused himself and followed the remaining uniforms towards the elevator. Closing the door behind them, Heidi turned towards Jerome, and found him already watching her.

"I can help you clean up," she offered lamely, finding it too difficult to explain her real reason for wanting to be near them.

He shook his head and strode fiercely across the floor towards her, but Heidi held her ground.

"Please..." She began, as he drew closer. He silenced her by reaching out to pull her into his arms, tucking her head beneath his chin and just holding her tight.

"Thank you," he gave a throaty growl against her hair. "Thank God you were here, and not that air-headed nanny."

It took Heidi a moment to respond. Her entire body had gone up in flames the moment he'd touched her. Shivery thrills of pleasure were racing through her veins, speeding up her heartbeat, and making it difficult to catch her breath.

Desire and joy washed away all fear. She felt so happy and safe in his arms, she never wanted to leave. But all too soon he was pulling back, just enough to urge her eyes up to meet his.

"You're... welcome..." She managed to respond, then glanced towards the boys, who were all three staring with wide eyes and cereal spoons suspended in curiosity. With his monk's attitude towards dating, they probably didn't see their father embracing very many women.

Heidi wanted to press her cheek back up against the hard, protective warmth of his chest, but Jerome had seen the boys' expressions as well. He gave a soft sigh, which almost sounded like regret. Then his jaw tensed and he slowly pulled away from her.

"Alright guys, it's long past your bedtime. We'll clean up this mess in the morning."

For one wrenching moment, Heidi nearly reached out to snatch Jerome back.

The terror was over. The reports would be filed and the criminals charged. But the desire which had brought her to his door at the beginning of this nightmare, had not changed. Only her perspective on dating a man with children was altered.

She wanted to spend more time with the boys, to assure that they had the support and understanding of an adult who had been through what they had just experienced. She cared for them now. All of them.

"Jerome?"

He had started following the direction the boys had taken, down the hall. Obviously, he'd expected her to simply see herself out. Now he glanced back, a strange blend of curiosity and confusion flickering across his eyes.

The air felt heavy all around her, a waiting silence, which was broken by the sound of water running and the boys noisily brushing their teeth.

Jerome was waiting for her to say something. Perhaps for her to explain why she was still standing in his living room, rather than walking out the front door to go home. But her words were caught behind a nervous tension that closed her throat and made speech impossible.

This was entirely unlike her. She'd never been afraid to speak her mind, often to the horror of her past boyfriends. But Jerome was different. She wanted to be with him more than she'd ever wanted to be with anyone else.

His gaze cut towards the open bathroom door, where it sounded as if the boys were having a rather loud gargling and spitting competition. Then he turned and slowly walked back across the floor to stand before her.

If she'd thought her nerves were frazzled before, this new proximity had them coming undone. Hope, fear, desire and excitement battled within her heart, sending electric shocks of pleasure and anticipation tickling down through her body. Down to ever fingertip and toe.

Goosebumps prickled along her skin and her breath began to come in little pants.

She licked her lips, and watched as his eyes captured the motion, darkening with awareness. Yet still he made no move to touch her, and she could not bring herself to reach for him.

His gaze finally rose to meet hers, but his expression was guarded, his emotions well hidden. He only waited, forcing her to summon up words that refused to be uttered. Yet just as she was preparing to surrender, he spoke first.

"Would you like to stay the night?"

Her heart eagerly skipped up into her throat, knocking free the barrier of fear that had hindered her voice. While at the same time, she felt her knees give a little shake beneath her, warning that she was now holding her breath and might faint if she didn't regain some composure.

"Yes," she gasped a bit breathlessly, then offered a slight frown as she considered the potential for misunderstanding. "But as much as I love the boys, I won't stay in that horrible little room you reserve for the nanny."

He gave a husky chuckle, before reaching out to trace his thumb over her lower lip in a gesture that awakened a whirling, fluttery heat low in her belly, and nearly sent her swooning into his arms.

"No," he assured her, in low and dangerously sexy murmur. "You'll be sleeping with me."

* * *

Heidi lay in Jerome's arms, with his body hard and strong against her back. She could feel his breath feathery and hot upon her cheek, and it sent a delicious shiver racing down her spine, despite all the wicked ways they had shared the last few hours.

He was everything she had dreamed he would be. Literally.

She smiled into the darkness that surrounded them, tracing a fingertip along the length of the powerful thigh pressed tight to the back of hers.

She felt the muscles tighten and ripple beneath the surface and her smile broadened.

"I dreamed of this," she murmured. "After you left, I slept in your bed, and I dreamed of being with you."

He tensed a little before answering.

"Would you be upset if it wasn't a dream?"

Heidi felt her smile slip.

"I might be a little peeved that you stole away again in the middle of the night, to let me deal with those two assholes alone," she growled, but made no move to leave his embrace. "So now might be a good time for you to explain a few things. After you tell me how you'd never intentionally put the boys or me in danger."

"I wouldn't," he rumbled with a fierceness that pleased her. "I received a call, alerting me to the Svalski's being in town. But I was told they were targeting my partner's family. I immediately left to protect them. Unfortunately, our Intel was incomplete. They were targeting us both and choose to hit here first."

Heidi rolled onto her back, to better see his shadow-cloaked face.

"Those men called you a Fed."

She felt, more than saw, him nod.

"I've been an agent for over twelve years."

"Isn't that dangerous, for a man with kids?"

"It was easier before Jane passed away," he admitted. "But the boys are just as safe as any judge or police officer's child."

He sighed and shook his head before continuing.

"There are a lot of bad people out there, but few are actually willing to hurt a child. Not even the Svalski's. I'm sure they would have let the boys go after they had me."

"They sure didn't have any qualms about knocking me around," she muttered.

He made another of those low growls, which she found both frightening and arousing.

"If I'd known that, I wouldn't have let them off with a couple of black eyes and bloody noses."

She frowned.

"You beat them up? When? How? They were in police custody before you arrived."

He abruptly rolled off the bed and padded barefoot across the ruins left behind by the Svalski brothers, to turn on the bedroom light.

Surprised, and half blinded by the sudden glare, Heidi sat up.

There was tension and grim determination in the way he was moving, warning her that the conversation had just taken an unexpectedly somber turn.

"There's something we need to discuss, before this gets too serious," he rumbled darkly.

"Stop right there," she warned. "This may have started as a fling, but I really care for you and the boys. If you're about to tell me this is just going to be a one-night stand, you better be ready for a fight."

He offered an amused, lopsided smile, and raised both palms to silence her.

"Let me rephrase," he urged in a voice which barely disguised a laugh. "Even if I still wanted to stop what's happening between us, I don't think I could. I'm so damned crazy about you, I might not ever let you out of that bed."

She had to force her mouth to close. That was about the last thing she'd expected him to say.

"But there is something we need to clear up first," he continued, once more dropping into that dour tone, which sounded as if he were about to scold her or admit to murder. "As I was putting the boys to bed, they told me what happened, just before I arrived."

For a moment, she was confused. Then she recalled Grizzly's meaty paw closing over the handle of his gun and the sudden appearance of hissing, spitting fur balls where the triplets had been seated.

"Jerome, I can explain," she gasped, as dread forced her to speak first. "I thought I could help the boys find strength and comfort in each other. It was just an innocent meditation ritual. I don't know what went wrong."

Now he looked confused, but she hurried on with her explanation, not giving him a chance to interrupt.

"I think it must have been the fear and horror of being held captive again. That and a need to keep the boys safe. It was an accident, I swear. I won't put them into such danger again. I'll talk to my coven, and we'll figure out what happened. But on the upside, the effects were only temporary."

He just stood there, staring at her.

Feeling suddenly exposed and uncomfortable, she pulled the bed sheet up to cover her naked body. But he only continued to look at her in that strange, dumbfounded manner.

"Jerome? Please, say something. You have to know that I would never intentionally cast a spell like that on the boys."

He shook his head, as if struggling to find his way through a blinding barrage of unspoken questions.

"Okay, so... Wait... What? Go back," he sputtered, obviously struggling over her explanation of the event. She couldn't really blame him. Chances were, he hadn't believed the boys when they'd told of how she'd turned them all into kittens. Now he was probably thinking they'd all been drugged or something.

"You're a witch?" He finally managed to grab hold of at least one of the questions spinning around inside his head.

She gave a tiny nod, wishing she could read his mind. Was he imagining green skin and warts? Or naked druids dancing in the trees?

Different people had different ideas about what made a modern witch. This sort of confession could destroy such a fragile new relationship. Possibly beyond repair.

"I'm a good witch," she offered the same assurance she'd given his sons. But it sounded ridiculous now and she immediately regretted it. She would have rambled on in a futile attempt to recover the situation, but he abruptly started laughing.

Instantly her temper flared.

It was one thing for him to disbelieve or challenge her lifestyle. But it was just downright rude for him to ridicule her.

"You know, I'm beginning to wish I did know how to cast that kitten transformation spell on command. It might come in handy when confronted by laughing hyenas," she snarled with a glower.

Jerome only laughed harder.

Yet just as she was considering shoving him out of the bedroom and locking the door behind him, he began to change.

It happened so quickly; she could only stare in amazement. One moment he was standing there making a guffawing ass out of himself. The next moment he was staring up from the bedroom floor, purring loudly.

For all that was holy!

She'd done it again. She'd turned Jerome into a large golden cat. An exact twin of the feline she'd seen in the elevator, just before...

"Oh my goddess!" She watched as the big cat gave a long, hard stretch. But it stretched longer and larger than any normal feline could. His body grew and hardened once more into the familiar figure of a man.

"You're a werewolf!"

"A shifter yes, but not a wolf," he corrected. "The boys inherited the gift from me, but their mother was a human, like you."

"Oh my goddess," she breathed again.

He waited for her to say more, but she wasn't really sure of where to begin. She had too many questions. If she hadn't already seen the boys change, she wasn't sure if she could have handled this sort of revelation.

"Does it hurt?" She finally managed.

"No more than performing a complicated yoga form," he grinned. "It comes naturally when practiced regularly, but you can see why I don't invite a lot of women to share my life. Most women would find it difficult sharing a life with someone like me and the boys. The little guys sometimes forget how disconcerting shifting might be for others."

That reminded her of the huge cat palace in the boys' room, and of the day she'd seen one of the triplets chasing two yellow kittens in the hall.

When the triplets had changed to escape the Svalskis, she'd been under too much stress to recognize that they were the same kittens she'd seen before.

"You know, I'm kind of surprised I didn't figure it out before," she admitted. "Maybe I would have, if given a little more time."

"I'm sure you would have," Jerome agreed. "Which is why I wanted to talk to you about it now. I want you to know what you'd be getting into, if you decide to give this relationship thing a chance."

She thought about that for a moment, before grinning.

"If you think you can live with a witch, then I think I can manage an occasional furball."

Heat and pleasure flashed in his eyes.

"Good, because I'd hate to be accused of kidnapping, and I really wasn't about to let you go."

He gave her a very predatory grin and began to stalk back across the floor.

Heidi couldn't help smiling as she let the sheet slip back down to pool around her waist.

"Bring it on, Tiger," she challenged, just before he

pounced.

ABOUT THE AUTHOR

Celeste Hall lives in the shadow of the Rocky Mountains and is a passionate writer and reader of romance novels. Her favorite stories include elements of paranormal or fantasy, but they always have a romantic heart.

To learn more about Celeste and her writing, please visit www.CelesteHall.com

The Seduction Series

A scorching hot paranormal erotic romance series by

CELESTE HALL

The Seduction Series follows an ongoing storyline and is best read in the following order...

- ETHAN
- KYE
- RICO
- GAVIN
- ALL THE QUEENS MEN
- THE BROTHERS SIN
- IAN
- LIAM

Stories of the incubus have been around since early history. Living in coveys made up of one queen and numerous males, they survive by feeding upon the sexual energy of sleeping humans. But these are no ordinary incubi, and they have thrown away the rulebook to bring human women home with them.

Warning: This series has violence and sexually explicit scenes with multiple partners. It is intended for mature adults eighteen years or older.

The Kitty Coven Series

A New Adult shapeshifter romance series by

Celeste Hall

This series can be read as standalone stories, but are best read in the following order...

- The Bare Witch Project
- Something Wicca This Way Comes
- Love is a Witch
- A Yowling Yuletide
- Cheaper by the Coven
- The Cat in the Hat

It all started on a cold October's eve in 1954. That's when a group of young witches cast a powerful spell that would forever change their lives and the lives of everyone in the small town of Aspire, New York.

Although there is some shapeshifter related nudity and suggestive situations, these are relatively clean romance novels written for mature teens and young adults.

SAVAGE THRONE

A passionate historical romance series by

CELESTE HALL

The Savage Throne Series follows an ongoing storyline, so it is best read in the following order...

In a savage land, ruled by a barbaric king, it is the innocent who suffer the most. A few fierce warriors still fight to protect the people from horde invasions, and from the often-cruel whims of the nobles.

Warning: This series has violence and sexual content that is intended for mature adults eighteen years or older.

Also by Celeste Hall

Lady Silence

Prison of Dreams

Simple Musings

His Pale Prisoner

Error: Please Try Again

Secret Admirer

The Inventors Throne

A Touch of Irish

Their First Time

Beware of Wolves

The Red Shoes

Sexy Shorts

For a current list of all books and short stories, please visit www.CelesteHall.com

Printed in Great Britain
by Amazon